THE MISTRESS
OF ORION HALL

THE MISTRESS OF ORION HALL

CLAUDETTE NICOLE

CUTTING EDGE

ISBN-13: 978-1-957868-11-0

Published by
Cutting Edge Books
PO Box 8212
Calabasas, CA 91372
www.cuttingedgebooks.com

CHAPTER ONE

*"The world was so made that certain
signs come before certain events."*
—CICERO

THE MISTRESS OF ORION HALL was dead. In the hanging
hours of the night they killed her. While the sea moaned
and flung itself against the land, she was slain. While the clouds
hurried to hide the face of the moon and the night owls covered
their yellow eyes with brown-feathered wings, the Mistress of
Orion Hall was slain. While the night sounds crept and crawled,
it was done.

But that was long ago. Or was it only yesterday?

The ash-gray fog had shrouded the night when she was
killed. In the chill damp of the dark she had gone out to prowl
the blackest shadows of the night. And death had finally met her
to claim its reward. Before the *meltemi* blew from the north to
tear away the veil of fog, it was over, and the Mistress of Orion
Hall was dead.

But that was long ago. Or was it only yesterday?

In masked and shrouded hoods they came for her, trembling
as they heard her laughter wild and terrible as an eagle's scream.
But there was no turning back or they would be lost forever, and
so her killers pressed on till the moment came and she lay dead.
Only then did they realize that in death she had cheated them of

their victory, and they fled into the darkness, sick with horror for themselves and for those yet to come.

When she was killed, it is said, the pomegranates turned bitter, the ripe black olives shriveled and fell from their branches, and the fruit of the lemon trees turned brown. The clouds held the moon for twenty-one nights and the seabirds wailed continuously for a hundred-and-one days.

But to some that was long, long ago. To those touched by it, it was only yesterday.

Sometimes yesterday can be just so much ancient history, especially when you've just turned twenty-two, when you're thoroughly and completely tingling with excitement and the world is popping open all around you like so many champagne corks. At least that's how it seemed to Lisa Bowen as she swung down from the big, red London bus and began to walk slowly across Trafalgar Square toward the hotel. Wearing her own very mini red dress, Lisa was conscious of the admiring glances, glad of her ability to hold her own with the long-stemmed English girls. She had spent most of the day sight-seeing and pinching herself to make certain it wasn't all a dream. She'd arrived in London a day early and now she tried to sort out the nearly unbelievable rush of events of the past forty-eight hours. First, of course, there had been the cablegram from Maggie. It had burst upon the quiet of the little white house in Middlebury, Vermont, with the force of a small nuclear blast. "Maggie" was really her aunt Margaret but she'd always been just Maggie to Lisa, and now the girl saw herself reading the wire aloud, her mother standing across the kitchen table from her.

DEAR LISA, BIG THINGS AFOOT. NEED SOMEONE WHO KNOWS GREEK. WHY GO ELSEWHERE WHEN BEST GREEK

HONORS STUDENT AT BENNINGTON WAS MY OWN NIECE.
PACK AT ONCE. MEET ME HOTEL EXCELSIOR, LONDON. AM
WIRING MONEY FOR PLANE FARE. WILL EXPLAIN WHEN I SEE
YOU. LOVE, MAGGIE.

Lisa recalled how her mother had been almost as excited as she. Since Daddy had died a little less than a year ago it had been a quiet house and her mother had urged Lisa to take a trip and get away. But there'd been a lot of unpaid debts, the estate to work out, and it just hadn't seemed the right time. And now this wonderful wire from Maggie.

"I wonder what it's all about," her mother had said, helping her pack.

"I don't much care," Lisa had laughed. "It'll be exciting and wonderful, whatever it is."

The scene faded from her mind as she passed through the lobby doors of the hotel. A pause at the desk brought the news that Miss Margaret Simpson of Sussex had indeed arrived and was in room 1601. Lisa hurried to catch the elevator just before the old-fashioned, ornate, grilled door closed. The "lift," as the English always called them, was maddeningly slow in its ascent. Lisa was excited just at the thought of seeing Maggie again. Aunt Margaret used to visit the family in Vermont twice a year with unfailing regularity. Lisa was a little girl growing up then, and there was always breathlessly exciting talk of London, Paris, Geneva, of other worlds she had only met in her school geography books. But as the years went on the visits grew less frequent and finally stopped altogether. But Maggie's wonderful letters kept coming—letters that were warm and witty and wise. She was one of those people who wrote letters just as she spoke and her sweeping personality leaped from the pages.

The lift halted and two men got on. Lisa smiled inwardly as their eyes paused to take in her beauty. Maggie would be surprised at her slim, grown-up loveliness, she knew. The last time Maggie had seen her she was a young, leggy pre-teen shooting out and up in all directions, uncoordinated as a baby colt. Her heart began to pound again as she thought of how so much had happened so quickly and she heard her mother's parting comment at the airport: "Aren't you glad now that you took Greek as a second language in school?" Her mother had laughed and Lisa had nodded vigorously. It had really been an off-hand choice, almost as a lark, because her father's grandmother had been half Greek. But, she recalled it had fallen easily to her tongue, amazingly easily. And she had enjoyed every bit of her Greek studies, all the things so many others found heavy. It had all come smoothly to her—the language, the culture, the history, the dark Greek dramas of Sophocles and Euripedes, the bright comedies of Menander and Aristophanes. She'd won honors and starred every year in the Bennington Greek Drama Society productions. With her dark-brown eyes, the straight, thin nose patrician and elegant, her way of carrying herself with a kind of proud serenity, she made an ideal heroine. Then she wore her hair long and hanging full instead of in her usual manner, pulled back in a semi-ponytail or combed upwards in back as it was now. And now, as she thought back, now it was all of real, practical importance to her. It was indeed a funny world full of totally unexpected things. Like the man outside the front door of the hotel when she'd arrived yesterday, dressed in a short jacket and high black boots. His eyes were deep caverns in a lined face and he had stared at her as though he couldn't believe what he saw, though she'd never set eyes on him before in her life. It gave her a strange sensation, not fright, not even uneasiness, but wonder. She'd remember that lined, craggy face. But she dismissed the incident quickly. A totally unexpected adventure should have unexpected pieces in it.

The lift stopped at the sixteenth floor and she stepped out, feeling the eyes of the men in the car follow the rounded upturned line of her breasts. She walked down the hall and quickly found room 1601. Maggie answered the door, paused for a long moment, and then gathered the girl in her arms in warm, encompassing delight. After crushing Lisa to her, the older woman pushed the girl back at arm's length and surveyed her.

"My God but you've grown into something lovely," Maggie said. Lisa laughed appreciatively. Maggie looked older than she'd remembered her; that was to be expected; there was a tiredness about her aunt's face, a weariness that had set in. She was still a commanding woman, though, a big, regal lady with that difficult-to-define quality called "presence." When Maggie entered a room, one knew she was there. It was, Lisa knew, the kind of thing that resulted from a combination of circumstances—a certain natural quality, a background of breeding and wealth, a life devoted to position and comforts. Maggie gestured to a couch in the hotel room and Lisa sat down. Her aunt produced a bottle of sherry from a suitcase and was pouring two small glasses. She handed one to Lisa and raised hers in a toast.

"To the new Mistress of Orion Hall," she said. "Does that mean anything at all to you, my dear?"

Lisa frowned and her mind plunged backwards to pick up bits and snippets of family talk she had heard over the years.

"I think so," she said tentatively. "Isn't that the old house that's been in the family for a hundred years or more?"

"That's right, my dear," Maggie said. "Unused, untouched, practically forgotten for so long."

"And it's on an island somewhere, right?" Lisa asked, feeling excitement growing inside her.

"On the island of Cyprus," Maggie said. "I'll tell you all about it, or at least all I know, seeing as I can't really do what I want to do without your help, in more ways than one."

Maggie poured another sherry for Lisa and herself and settled back on the couch. "I've decided to open up Orion Hall," she said. "To go there and live out the rest of my days."

Lisa kept her eyebrows from raising but she couldn't help but wonder at this decision.

"I've heard that Cyprus, in the eastern Mediterranean, is a delightful island," Maggie said. "Slow-moving, wonderful climate, a thoroughly leisurely place." Lisa nodded but her aunt's words did not satisfy her as an explanation.

"Orion Hall has been shrouded in legend," Maggie continued. "I've heard all sorts of half stories but the only hard facts I've been able to gather I've gotten from going over old deeds and family papers. It was built by your great-grandfather on your father's side, Richard Willis, for the Greek girl he married. He was a wealthy young man, a student on the island of Rhodes in the Aegean, when he met this girl, Athena. It seems he fell in love with her and married her at once. She wanted him to build a house for her on Cyprus and he built Orion Hall. They lived there for a time and then he died very suddenly. According to what I've learned, Athena stayed on as Mistress of Orion Hall until she was killed in an accident of some kind a good number of years later. But before Richard Willis died there was a child. She was sent to England to live and be educated. From England she went to America and never set foot on Cyprus again."

"That would be Grandmother Willis," Lisa interjected, pulling on her memory of family talk again.

"Exactly," Maggie said. "She made a life in America and never looked backwards, it seemed. After Athena, the last Mistress of Orion Hall and the only one, was killed in the accident, the house remained unoccupied. From what I've been able to gather, Richard Willis was somewhat of a family black sheep and nobody wanted any part of the place. Then there were the wars that followed which kept my part of the family busy for jolly old England in India, Burma, Europe, and all over the world. In more recent times Cyprus revolted for independence and developed quite an anti-British atmosphere. It was a sticky business and, of course, no one wanted to go there then. But that's all over now; Cyprus is an independent state. All the old papers were amassed on my side of the family, probably because my uncle Harold was executor for the family. A month ago, when I made my decision to go there and become the new tenant, I put all the old papers in some sort of order. Now, in actuality, you are genealogically the remaining blood descendant of the Mistress of Orion Hall, Lisa."

"Me?" Lisa frowned. Maggie nodded. "And your mother, of course," she added. "But as you are the last descendant, I'm told that to keep everything legal and proper you have to sign these papers allowing me to take over Orion Hall and live there."

Maggie reached behind to a table and picked up a briefcase. She took a sheaf of legal-looking papers from it and handed them to the girl. "They're drawn so that when I'm gone Orion Hall will automatically go back to you, my dear."

Lisa found her pen in her purse and signed the papers without a second look at them. It gave her a warm, satisfying feeling to be able to do something for Maggie, to partially repay all those years of visits and gifts. She handed them back to the older woman.

"Thank you, my dear," Maggie said simply.

"I think it's wonderful and exciting of you to include me in all this," Lisa said with sincerity, her brown eyes sparkling.

"You'll earn every minute of it," Maggie laughed. "I'll need you to translate for me and to teach me enough Greek so someday

I can get around on my own. Though Cyprus is an independent state, it is basically Greek. The population is about eighty-five percent Greek. The other fifteen percent is primarily Turkish. And, like all the Greek islands, it is more Greek than Greece—more insulated, more steeped in tradition and superstition."

Maggie suddenly cast a glance at her watch and rose abruptly, draining her sherry. "That lawyer fellow," she said, a grim, angry tone creeping into her voice. "I've got to get across town and I want you to come with me."

"Trouble?" Lisa asked, and was sorry she'd been so quick to intrude. But Maggie only snorted.

"Not really," she said. "Just some rather fast operators, I suspect. Orion Hall is at one end of a small village called Caramania and I was informed that local law requires a notice of intended residency to be given, especially in the case of foreigners. I sent notice off to the mayor of the village. Since then I've received four crude letters, unsigned, warning me not to come to Orion Hall. Then last week I received a letter from a barrister here in London, a Mr. Al Burton. His letter claims he has a client who put a down payment on Orion Hall and this was in order because of unpaid back taxes on the place. He suggests I wait six months before proceeding with any residency plans because his client will be away till then."

"And you think that's all in error?" Lisa asked.

"It's more than an error," Maggie snapped. "This lawyer fellow's approach is just a more clever variation of the four crude, anonymous letters. I daresay some smart operators have been working some kind of racket, probably renting out rooms in Orion Hall to tourists. Naturally my going to live there will end what is undoubtedly a lucrative little sideline. But that is precisely what I intend to do."

Lisa got up and followed Maggie as she swept out of the room and into the hall. The elevator was just coming down and they caught it and were out on the street in moments. Maggie took a small card from her purse. "This was attached to his letter," she said, waving down a high-roofed London cab with tall windows.

"Twelve Dexter Street," Maggie commanded. Lisa enjoyed London as they rode across the city and Maggie seemed occupied with her own thoughts. Lisa cast quick glances at the older woman and detected that faint weary expression lurking just behind her eyes. Or was it worry? No, she decided, it was more a kind of sadness. Probably Maggie was sad at leaving old friends and her beloved England. But why go then, she wondered again. There *was* an unquestionable sadness in the woman's eyes when, in moments of repose like this, the bright twinkle of her personality rested. Lisa turned away. It had always been too easy for her to plunge into melancholy. "That's the Greek in you," her father would say when someone else's sadness reached out to wrap itself around her. The girl was glad to feel the taxi come to a halt.

She swung long, smooth legs out of the door, legs that caused two workmen repairing a street lamp to stop and watch. This was the East End section of London, a part of it she hadn't seen and didn't want to see again. It hadn't the angry vitality of an American slum. It was just steeped in grayness—a bleak, numbing sort of place with stone houses that clung to each other defensively in stair-step rows. Maggie was looking up at a ground floor window, a dirty, grimy window, and Lisa saw the lawyer's card stuck in one corner.

"Hardly one of the Queen's barristers, Mr. Al Burton," Maggie said dryly. "Let's have it over with, shall we?"

Lisa drew up behind her aunt as they mounted the few steps and rang a painfully loud bell. Someone buzzed back and the door opened. They entered a dingy, dark hallway of old wallpaper and dark, unpolished woodwork. A small man, olive-skinned, with darting brown eyes and a ferretlike face, waved them into a ground floor office, poorly lighted, perhaps to hide the general shoddiness of it. Maggie sat down in a chair before a small desk. Lisa perched on a straight-backed chair near her aunt. The little man's eyes were shrewd and cold, with a flat, deadly quality to them despite their brightness. She almost felt her skin crawl as his eyes lingered on her, taking in her beauty. It was like being gone over by a snake. Maggie began things in her usual, abrupt, imperious way. She opened the briefcase and drew out a sheaf of papers and waved them in the lawyer's face.

"Your client, my good man, if he really exists and if he has indeed put a down payment on Orion Hall, has been very much misled," Maggie said, her tone clipped, impatient. "These papers record the tax payments made on Orion Hall over the past seventy years. There is no tax liability unpaid and your client has no claims whatever."

Mr. Burton shrugged and didn't seem to be at all bothered. He tried a small, coldly mechanical smile.

"I did not handle those negotiations," he said. "I have only been retained recently and can only state what I was told. I am also informed that the place is virtually without water and that the old wells have dried up. It is in terrible need of repair, too."

Maggie's eyes speared the little man. "The Willis estate paid a family in the village to maintain general repairs over the years. A sum was paid them yearly and as the last member of the family died only two years ago, I doubt that the place is in terrible condition."

Maggie stood up and tossed the papers on the man's desk, giving him a withering glance of contempt at the same time.

"I don't know what your little game is, or who put you up to it, but I don't expect any further rubbish from you," she snapped. "Those are photostatic copies of the tax payments, just on the off chance that you should have some cretin of a client."

Turning abruptly, Maggie was half out the door before Lisa hurriedly caught up with her. Lisa shot a fast glance at the little man and saw the cold glitter of his narrowed eyes, the cruelty in the tight line of his mouth. She hurried after Maggie, glad to find herself out on the street.

"Of course they had nothing to lose by trying," Maggie said. "Perhaps someone else might have been scared off by anonymous letters and lawyer's talk of options and unpaid taxes. But they had the wrong person in Maggie Simpson."

Maggie was certain the thing was done with, over, nothing but a minor attempt at small-time chicanery. But Lisa felt there had been something latently deadly in the lawyer. She still held the image of the little man's eyes inside her mind and she had an unexplained, cold feeling of danger. Yet she shook it away. She refused to be a victim of silly imaginings.

"We'll go back to the hotel and wash him away with some good wine over dinner," Maggie said. "Whatever he is, I'm sure his name is not Mr. Al Burton. The man's an Arab if I ever saw one. Or possibly an Egyptian."

"You sound so certain," Lisa said.

"You forget I spent every winter in Morocco for five years," Maggie said. "You get to know the types. Al Burton, indeed. I'd say his name was more likely El-Boutani or some such thing."

Lisa laughed along with her aunt and they got another high-roofed cab back to the hotel. Over dinner Lisa learned that they would fly to Athens in the morning. Then they would leave from Piraeus, the seaport of Athens, go by boat to Cyprus, and land at the harbor port of Kyrenia. Even the good, thick roast beef and a fine bottle of Chambertin burgundy couldn't dull the edge of the mounting excitement inside her.

When the long, leisurely dinner was over and she was back in her room, she drew a hot bath and relaxed in it. As the warmth of the water curled around her, Lisa reflected that she must be about the luckiest girl in the world. Not that she'd had a hard life. There had been a few lean years but her father had always managed to provide for the family and she had been given ample material advantages, such as the years at college. More important, she had known the good things of love and wisdom and security. Love. The word revolved in her mind. There had always been ardent and eager young men and she stretched, catlike, savoring the warmth of her memories. Love had always been something of a problem to her, a problem of her own making. It was her nature to respond openly, freely, trustingly, to involve herself with other people's needs. But she'd learned not to give so fully of herself, physically and emotionally. It had been hard learning. It had taken a lot of hurts to realize that giving is too often a one-way street. And so she had learned to hold back, a little, anyway. But she was still vulnerable to stray cats, to those who used needing as a weapon. And, she admitted to herself, she was still an incurable romanticist, helplessly drawn by the pleasures and pains of the emotions. That, too, her father used to say, was the Greek in her, that inclination toward the tragic in happiness, the darkness inside the light. But she had always held that it was merely the result of being a small-town girl. Even going to college at Bennington hadn't taken her out of Vermont. Dreams of faraway places and exciting adventures had been no more than that, lived vicariously through Maggie's visits when Lisa was a little girl and through her letters afterwards. And now she was doing those very things she'd come to be sure would never be more than dreams. Lisa got out of the bath, drying herself slowly, luxuriating in the sensuousness of her lovely body. Wrapping a towel around her, she went to bed, still marveling at how completely life had turned around for her in the last few days. She went to sleep to hurry the coming day.

In the morning Lisa was up early, putting on a McCleod tartan minikilt and a soft-yellow jersey blouse. She went to Maggie's room and found her aunt also packed and ready to go.

"I'll be glad to be settled and secure again," Maggie said over coffee and once more Lisa wondered what the remark, almost absent-mindedly tossed out, really meant. She had always thought of Maggie as secure and settled. She felt her aunt's hand press down over hers and she looked up to see Maggie's eyes, grave and warm, looking at her.

"I'm so very glad you could come with me on this venture, my dear," Maggie said. "You don't know what a comfort you've been already. And you'll be more of one, I know."

Lisa smiled back and felt good. It was almost strange to think of herself as being a comfort to Maggie. Her aunt wasn't one of those women who ever seemed to need comforting. She always seemed in charge of herself and everything around her. And in truth, she most always was. But, Lisa was learning, there are few people so self-contained as to be without need of human companionship and understanding. Time prevented further reflection as Maggie hurried them both through breakfast and they gathered their bags for the trip to the airport. The flight itself from London to Athens was uneventful and thoroughly routine. It was only when they hurried through Athens to Piraeus and to the little dock overcrowded with people that Lisa began to get the taste and smell and feel of her destination.

There were many women on the dock, mostly in black kerchiefs and shawls, carrying burlap traveling bags, some with small chickens in wooden boxes. The women were short, for the most part, without makeup, their faces severe, unsmiling. The dock was almost awash with tears and there was much loud wailing and fervent embracing. Lisa saw a smattering of students and some men, stern-faced, in work clothes with short-brimmed caps. The steamer itself was small, old, and definitely no tourist boat. Later Lisa learned it was the only steamer to the island. They pushed their way through the crowd to rest their bags near the gangplank. Overhead a cargo crane on the forward deck of the ship was still swinging huge nets filled with crates and heavy machinery from the dock into open hatches. Lisa watched it as it swung slowly over the crowded dock, a giant claw of rope with its contents inside. Her eyes moved from the crane to sweep the dock and she frowned. There, on the far side, was the cavernous-eyed man with the gaunt, lined face she had seen outside the hotel that first day she arrived. Or was it the same man? He wore the same high boots and short dark jacket and she thought she would never mistake those burning, deep eyes. But there were other men with high, shiny boots, their faces also lined, their hair black and curly, too. She couldn't really be sure and she looked away. Many of the people were starting to go on board when she saw the gypsy woman in a corner of the pier, sitting before a canvas with a huge eye painted on it, a small knot of people gathered around her. She sat on a pile of old matting and turned cards over for some, looked at the palm of others, and just muttered to a few.

"Do we have time for me to have my fortune told?" Lisa asked Maggie, pressing her hand on the older woman's arm. "I've always wanted to have it done by a real gypsy."

"She's real enough," Maggie said. "Probably a lot more real than her cackling fortunes."

"I've just got to talk to her," Lisa said excitedly, elbowing her way toward the woman. The gypsy woman wore a red bandanna that only partially covered jet-black hair. She had on a scoop-necked, red silk blouse that lay flat against huge, pendulous breasts. Her face was both aged and ageless, old when she smiled an uneven smile, surprisingly young when she studied the cards that lay in the lap of her wide skirt. Her skin was olive-hued, the cheeks smooth, but her eyes were surrounded by hundreds of tiny wrinkles. Of course she'll see me as a tourist, Lisa told herself. She'll trot out her most shopworn routines but I don't care, she thought. This was something Lisa had always wanted to do, ever since the days when she used to go to the fake gypsies that traveled with the small, backwoods circuses in the rural Vermont areas. An old woman moved away and Lisa found herself standing behind a short, white-haired man who was next in line. The gypsy woman muttered some words to the old man and he moved off. The woman gazed at Lisa from behind half-veiled eyes that traveled up and down her figure. Lisa dropped a few coins into the woman's lap as she had seen others do. The gypsy woman continued to stare at her through half-lowered lids.

"Do you have any wisdom for me?" Lisa asked.

"You go to Kyrenia," the gypsy said and Lisa frowned. How did the woman know that? The ship made other stops. A guess, no doubt, she answered herself. Most tourists stopped there, probably.

"I will sing you a song," the gypsy woman said. "An old Turkish song."

She began to sing, her voice soft, steady, with almost a lullaby quality to it. The singing was more a cadenced speaking with measured changes of pitch and there was a strange edge inside the softness of it.

> *If you should go to Kyrenia,*
>   *Don't enter the walls.*
> *If you should enter the walls,*
>   *Don't stay long.*
> *If you should stay long,*
>   *Don't get married.*
> *If you should get married,*
>   *Don't have children.*

She stopped as suddenly as she had begun and turned away. Lisa felt a coldness in the pit of her stomach. She watched the gypsy woman disappear behind the canvas with the big eye on it and she turned away. The song had been slight, strange, and yet it seemed to say more than the words itself said. It was a warning, a verse of hidden meanings, and it lay curled up inside her like some unwelcome bit of food, leaving a sour taste in her mouth. The crowd on the dock had thinned out now and she saw Maggie standing beside the bags near the gangplank. As she started toward her aunt, she saw the big cargo boom swing directly over Maggie, moving slowly. As she looked up at it, Lisa's eyes widened in horror. One end of the net was pulling loose. Inside, the heavy metal crate shifted, about to spill out as she stood transfixed, watching it. The end of the net came apart and the heavy crate started to fall. It had an unreal, slow motion, picture quality to it. Lisa screamed and Maggie turned to her, startled. The girl dived, catching the older woman about the waist, knocking her backwards and falling along with her.

As they hit the wooden planking of the dock, she heard and felt the thundering crash of the heavy crate as it smashed down on the spot where Maggie had been standing a second before. The dock trembled and then was still and in moments other hands were helping them both to their feet. Crewmen had dashed from the ship and the captain was there, too, his face dark with concern. Lisa also looked at Maggie with concern. It had been a hard fall. But the older woman was all right, merely shaken up a little.

"Thanks would sound so damned inadequate, my child," Maggie said, huffing herself up, straightening her dress. "I'll have to find some other way."

But Maggie's eyes had held their gratitude and the incident passed over as the captain escorted them both up to their cabins murmuring about fate and accidents. It had been one of those freak things that happen every once in a while, he explained, and it was the only logical, plausible explanation. Lisa wondered why she felt so unsatisfied by it. It was the gypsy woman's strange song still with her, unsettling and unnerving, she decided. In any case, no one had been killed, or even injured, and the captain had insisted they dine at his table for the evening meal, so all had turned out for the best. It was later, when she'd gotten settled into her cabin adjoining Maggie's, that she went to her aunt and spoke again of the near tragedy.

"A thing like that couldn't have happened on purpose, do you think, Maggie?" she asked. Maggie glanced at her with a tolerant frown.

"Now what in heavens makes you even think of something like that?" Maggie asked. "Really, now, my child."

"I don't know," Lisa shrugged. "I was just thinking about those anonymous warning letters you got and that Mr. Burton and someone not wanting you to go to Orion Hall."

"My, you do have an active imagination, don't you?" Maggie laughed. Lisa was glad she hadn't mentioned the man with the deep, cavernous eyes. She was already feeling ashamed of being so imaginative. Maggie's arm was around her shoulders steering her out onto the deck.

"Let's go out and watch the ship sail," she said. "One thing you can't do on Cyprus is let your imagination run away with you, I'm told. The place is full of legends and superstitions anyway. Accidents are accidents. Nobody can explain the strange workings of fate and why they happen to some people and not others. I say let's just forget about the whole thing."

It seemed to be a good idea. They stood by the rail as the little steamer pulled away from the dock. The blue waters of the Aegean sparkled as the little vessel began to nose its way through waters once sailed by the ships of Persian kings and Macedonian warriors. Lisa put aside thoughts of accidents and strange songs of gypsy women. It was better that way.

CHAPTER TWO

"The hardest crusts always
fall to the toothless."
—Cypriote Greek Proverb

Lisa spent most of the day at the ship's rail as the little vessel wound its way through the Greek islands, along the watery routes where Odysseus sailed to the adventures that Homer relates, where Paris sailed on his high-prowed ships with beautiful Helen of Troy, where western civilization was cradled. She delighted in picking out the different islands as the ship threaded its way through them: Mikonos; Delos, birthplace of Apollo; Crete, where St. Paul sought haven from the storm; Patmos, where John wrote the last Book of the Bible in exile; Rhodes, home of the Colossus and of scholarship—each of them a pearl in the necklace of western culture. Only when it grew dark and she could no longer make out the shapes of the islands strung out like footprints of history did she go to her cabin and change for dinner. Most of the other passengers were traveling in what was still called, in those waters, "steerage" and Lisa found that she, her aunt, and an elderly gentleman were the only ones besides the captain's staff in the dining salon. It was lucky at that, she decided, for the dining salon was hardly large enough for many more. They were midway through the meal when she noticed the little vessel had begun to roll and pitch with increasing severity.

"I am afraid we are in for bad weather," the captain said, a serious-faced man whose name was Karapoulis. "One of our violent and sudden Mediterranean storms. They blow in from the north. The island people call them the *meltemi*. Everyone must stay in their cabins until the storm is over." He finished his wine and his eyes took in each one of the travelers.

"There is nothing to worry about in regard to the ship," he said. "It may be very uncomfortable for a while as the ship will bob about like a cork. But she will stay afloat. The decks are something else again. They are extremely dangerous in a storm. Even my experienced crewmen move on them only if they must. So, please keep to your cabins."

He rose and motioned to the mate. "Please escort the two ladies to their cabins now," he said, bowing stiffly and turning on his heel to leave. Lisa stood up with Maggie and caught the edge of the table as the ship rolled suddenly, and then they both followed the ship's officer from the salon. The walk to the cabins was a short distance on the open deck and Lisa felt the sting of salt spray. She glimpsed a dark, towering wave rise up over the top of the ship's rail, making her feel very helpless and tiny. The mate held open for them the door that led to a short, inside corridor protecting the cabins. They half fell into the corridor and heard the door shut behind them.

"I think we'd best stay in our cabins," Maggie said as the ship lurched again. "I'll see you in the morning." Maggie waved a cheery good night and Lisa waited to see her disappear inside the cabin before going into her own. Alone, the girl took off her dress and lay down on the small bed in her bra and panties, turning off the lobe light that made her dizzy as it swayed and swung with every roll of the ship. In the darkness she listened to the sound of the sea punishing the sides of the little vessel, slamming its great fists into the steel and wood with thunderous regularity.

The rolling and pitching took on a rhythm of its own and she finally fell asleep. But it was a fitful sleep and she half woke with every pitch that was harder than the others. She didn't know how long she'd been asleep when she suddenly wakened to a cry, her name being called. It was Maggie's voice. Lisa sat up, listening. But there was only the sound of the sea and the wail of the wind. Had she imagined it, dreamt it? The wind could have played tricks with her sleeping mind. She heard the wind howl again and again a faint call. It was her name, she gasped silently. Or it sounded like it. She swung from the bed, threw on slacks and a blouse, and raced into the corridor. Water from the outside had come in under the corridor door and the floor was wet under her bare feet. She hurried to Maggie's room, paused at the door, and called to her aunt. There was no answer. Lisa opened the door. The cabin was empty and dark. Fright seizing her in its cold grip, she whirled and ran up the few steps to the door to the deck. There was nowhere in the short corridor Maggie could have gone except up onto the deck. Pressing her lips together with characteristic determination, Lisa pushed on the door and went out. A cascade of cold water struck her like a blow, flinging her against the outside wall of the cabin, bouncing her head hard against the wood. Her hand found the brass rail that ran along the cabin wall and closed around it. The ship pitched and the water drained from the deck in a rush. She rubbed her eyes dry with the back of one hand and peered across the deck through the darkness. There was a form clinging to the outside rail, prone, hanging on for dear life with both hands. It was Maggie, she saw, Maggie inches and seconds from being swept into the raging sea. The ship heaved and she saw a wall of water crash over the rail. It hit Maggie's form, jarring her grip loose. Maggie slid along the wet deck, pushed by the force of the water. This roll was carrying her in, toward the cabin, but Lisa knew that when the ship reversed its roll her aunt would be swept back over the rail and into the sea.

The girl let go of her grip on the brass railing, fell onto her stomach, and let herself slide across the deck toward Maggie. Could she reach the older woman in time, before the ship started to roll back the other way? Lisa clawed with her hands on the deck, trying to help the water as it swept her along. Water washed over her, pushing her on, spinning her sideways. The ship started to keel over to starboard. She saw Maggie begin to slide away from her. Pushing with her feet, getting enough leverage to half dive, half slide forward, Lisa got an arm out and felt her hand close around Maggie's wrist. She pulled hard and they both slid down the tilting deck. But Lisa counted on her added weight to keep them from being swept overboard. She was alongside Maggie now, getting a firmer grip on the older woman's arm. She saw the mountainous sea rearing up in dark green fury as the ship dipped its side into it. They were sliding hard now, into the rail. Lisa felt her body hit the ridge of the uprights on the rail and send her breath out in pain. She locked one arm around an upright and clung to it, her other arm tight around Maggie. She felt Maggie's hands gripping her waist. The rail dipped, the water rushed over them, and the sea pulled at them, trying to tear them away and into its surging grasp. But Lisa clung on, her arm hurting terribly, her muscles weakening. She felt Maggie slip off with one hand but the older woman still kept a grip with the other. "Hang on!" Lisa shouted as the rail started to come up out of the water. The sea that poured over them swept on, leaving only windblown spray stinging their soaked bodies. The ship was almost on an even keel, resting there for a long moment as the sea gathered itself for another assault.

"Come on," Lisa gasped, releasing her grip on the rail. They had perhaps thirty or forty seconds, she knew. On her knees she scrambled toward the center of the deck, Maggie following along clinging to the waist of her slacks. Through the driving rain and water Lisa saw the yellow square of light above from the ship's pilothouse. A flight of steps, a steep ladder, led to it from the deck. Lisa reached it, grabbing the lowest rung with both arms as the ship went into another sharp roll. Maggie landed against her and Lisa positioned her body to press the older woman against the wall. The sea swept over the rail again and washed over them but Lisa held her arms tightly locked around the lower step of the ladder. Her shoulder muscles cried out as the water pulled at her body and lifted her to press her hard against the sharp edge of the ladder. But she kept her hold and the sea swept back for another try. Desperation giving her the strength to scream, she cried out as the ship righted itself again. She screamed again and again and heard the pilothouse door open. In moments strong hands were lifting her up, pulling her into the warmth and light of the little pilothouse. She saw another seaman bringing Maggie in. The captain was there, beside the man at the ship's big wheel.

"What were you doing out on the deck in this storm?" he asked Lisa while a crewman propped Maggie's soaked form against one wall and gently massaged her face. Lisa was glad to see the semblance of color returning to her aunt's cheeks.

"I woke up and heard my aunt calling me," Lisa said. "I went to her cabin and she wasn't there. I heard her again and went outside."

"It's a miracle you weren't both swept overboard," Captain Karapoulis muttered. He looked down at Maggie. The older woman was breathing evenly but her eyes were still shut.

"I'll wait till later to question her," he said. "She's in a state of shock. Get some brandy." One of the crewmen reached into a drawer to one side and produced a flask. A little was poured into Maggie's mouth. Lisa saw her aunt cough, her eyes open, and then watched as the woman took in more small sips of the brandy. The captain peered out the window.

"The worst is past," he said. "You'll be able to return to your cabins soon." He fastened an eye on Maggie as two sailors lifted her to her feet. Maggie's eyes were still dazed and Lisa went to her side.

"What happened, Maggie?" the girl asked gently.

"I ... I'm not sure," Maggie said, shivering. Lisa's wet clothes were making her own skin run cold. The captain interrupted. "My men will take you to your cabins. Change into dry clothes at once," he said "I will come down soon and speak to you both then."

Lisa and Maggie were escorted down the ladder by two crewmen. The sea was still mountainous but the terrible wind had died down and the water, almost reluctantly, was only sweeping by the sides of the little vessel. Inside her cabin Lisa stripped quickly, dried her wet body, and donned a fresh pair of slacks and a sweater. She went to Maggie's cabin and her aunt opened the door, embracing the girl in a tight grip.

"Lisa, my dear, my dear," the older woman said. "Thanks to you I'm alive and not out there in the Mediterranean. Saving me is getting to be a habit."

Lisa laughed and stepped back. Maggie looked better; her eyes were back to their usual commanding blue with the dazed shock gone from them and she was warm in a wool robe.

"But what happened, Maggie?" Lisa asked, growing serious. "What were you doing out there anyway?"

Maggie's lips tightened. "I was asleep when someone knocked on my cabin door and called to me," she said. "I got up, put on a shift, and went outside. There was no one. Then I heard my name called again from outside on the deck. I followed the sound and no sooner opened the door to the deck when a wave knocked me off my feet. The rest is all a terrible jumble and nightmare. I called for you, I know, and you obviously heard me."

"What about the person that called you?"

"There was no one," Maggie said, her jaw tightening. "No one at all."

"What kind of a voice was it?"

Maggie passed a hand over her forehead. "It sounded like it could have been you," she said. "A high-pitched voice. I guess I was still partly asleep when I went outside."

Maggie looked at Lisa's frown and she nodded her head.

"Say what you're thinking, my child," she said.

"I really don't know what I'm thinking," the girl answered truthfully. "Are you sure someone called you?"

"I was sure, then," Maggie said. "I'd still say so. It's what I'll tell Captain Karapoulis. But in truth, my dear, I don't know, I just don't know. It could have been the wind, or a dream."

"A dream?" Lisa echoed. "Do you sleepwalk, Maggie?"

"No, not usually anyway," Maggie said gravely. "But it has happened, at times when I've been unusually tense and troubled. It could have happened tonight."

Maggie whirled and pounded her fist into her hand in exasperation. "Oh, I wish I could be sure of what it was," she said, "of what brought me out on that deck. I heard someone call me, that's definite."

"Then that's what it was," Lisa said. "But why and where did they go?"

Maggie's eyes were grave again. "You can hear a definite call in your mind, my dear," she said. "Even the wind can do it. But to you, when you hear it, it's real."

"I suppose so," Lisa said, pondering the thought. Maggie put her hand on the girl's shoulder. "You go back and get some sleep. It's been a difficult night and I'm sure you're more than a little sore."

Lisa had to smile in agreement. Her arms and shoulders ached and she was suddenly terribly tired. She said good night and went to her cabin. The ship was rocking almost gently now as she lay in the darkness of the cabin wondering where the truth lay in Maggie's words. What had made the woman venture out onto the storm-swept deck to certain death? The wind playing tricks with her sleep-filled mind? Her own mind hearing things that were real only to itself, being pulled on by the strange forces which pull on all sleepwalkers? Or had there been a voice cleverly calling Maggie to certain death, death which would have been an accidental tragedy at sea? The conflicting possibilities danced in her mind until sleep put an end to their disturbing carousel.

In the morning, after sleeping late, she dressed and found Maggie already taking in the warm sun in a chair on deck. It was so bright and cheerful that the night seemed something that had never happened. But the bruises on her ribs told her it had happened, all too real and frighteningly. It seemed ridiculous to voice her thoughts in the brilliant sunlight but she plunged on anyway.

"Suppose someone did call you out on deck last night, Maggie," Lisa said, sitting down next to her aunt. "You know what that would mean, don't you?"

"Suppose you spell it out for me, Lisa," Maggie answered, looking out at the water.

"It would mean someone tried to kill you and make it seem like just another shipboard accident," said Lisa. "A foolish woman who went out on deck during the storm."

"Why would anyone want to do that?"

"To keep you from opening Orion Hall?" Lisa suggested.

"You're still thinking of those warning letters and that lawyer trying to get me to stay away," Maggie said.

"I guess so," Lisa admitted.

"Nonsense, my dear," Maggie replied. "Nobody wants me away from Orion Hall enough to commit murder. I've been thinking a lot about last night and I've concluded I must have been sleepwalking. It's happened before, every time I've been under stress and strain for a long period. I'm afraid it was nothing more spectacular than that, my dear. The Greek in you certainly comes out in that imagination of yours, Lisa my girl."

Lisa sat silently, annoyed with herself for having brought it up.

"Stop leaning to the dark and devious, Lisa Bowen," Maggie said gently. "Walk around the ship, clear your mind, think of what fun we'll be having soon. It was one of those terrible things that turned out all right, largely thanks to you, but nothing more."

Lisa nodded, got up, and walked away. The water was a rich, calm blue and the sun so very warm and life giving. On the forward deck the main part of the passenger list milled about in noisy profusion. Lisa walked to the stem, sat down on the flat top of a deck cleat, and looked out at the sea. Had she been too quick to leap to the dark and devious, in Maggie's words? It was more than possible. She'd always been too quick to follow her emotions, too trusting of the wisdom of the heart. When she'd woken this morning all she could think of was that the accidents—first the crane and now this—were too coincidental. But, in truth, she had to admit that coincidences did exist and accidents often happened in threes. She would have to get hold of herself, she thought angrily. Logic, reason, not emotional flights of fancy, should color her thoughts, she told herself sternly. She leaned back against the railing and let the sun warm her and the gentle roll of the ship put her into a half sleep, curled up like a child in a corner. The cry of sea gulls woke her and she got up to see an island outlined ahead. Hurriedly she went down to her cabin, pausing at Maggie's open door.

"Cyprus," Maggie said. "Get your things together."

Lisa hurried to her cabin and packed quickly and soon she was crowding the rail beside Maggie, gazing excitedly at the harbor port of Kyrenia, as the little vessel nosed its way toward a low, wooden, unroofed pier. Beyond it, white-tiled houses with gray slate roofs rose up from the small, neat harbor. Whitewashed walls circled the ascending rows of houses and mounted the hillsides in an orderly progression. The words of the gypsy woman came back to her. Though the woman's song had spoken of Kyrenia, Lisa felt it was meant for far more than this one port, and its strange ominous quality remained with her. The vessel made fast and the disembarking passengers headed down the gangplank to the dock, Lisa following Maggie down with the others. One of her first acts, she decided, would be to find a book on the island and learn more about it. She disliked living somewhere and knowing little of the land's history. The swaying of the gangplank gave way to the firmness of the dock and Lisa gazed out to the stone street that bordered it. As she did so, she saw the man, his high boots carrying him from the dock to the street. He glanced back and she saw the gaunt face, the deep eyes. Was it the same man, she wondered. It certainly seemed so. Again she saw others with high boots and short dark jackets pass by. There was something unforgettable about him, even though the attire seemed to be common on Cyprus, along with deep eyes and strong, lined faces and glistening black hair.

"You stay here with the bags," she heard Maggie say. "I'll try to find us a taxi. We've a long trip to Caramania."

Lisa sat down on a suitcase and watched the men that passed on the sun-drenched street—big men, strong men, men who strode with their chests out, men with bodies that radiated an animal strength, a masculine sensuousness. She would say nothing to Maggie about the man, she decided, not unless something occurred that she could be certain was more than her imagination. Her thoughts were interrupted by a coughing, choking noise and she peered down the street to see Maggie's arm waving from the window of a battered vehicle that sputtered its way toward her. It moved in fits and starts as though it were a child's toy and Lisa found herself glancing at the rear of it to see if there wasn't a giant key extending out with which to wind it up. It was patched together with parts and pieces from a dozen other cars, no two alike it seemed, giving it the appearance of a metal patchwork quilt.

Maggie got out and the driver followed her and began putting their bags on a rickety roof rack. He was an impassive man with a large and flowing brown moustache. Lisa got into the rear of the taxi beside Maggie and they started off with a series of lurches.

"This thing will never make it to the end of town," Lisa whispered.

"He assured me he often drives to Caramania," Maggie said. "Anyway, it was the only one I could find."

To Lisa's surprise the chugging and lurching stopped when the driver shifted gears and gained more speed, and they began the drive along winding roads, mostly hugging the shoreline. Hillsides of olives, figs, and dates went by, brightened by spots of tangerine and lemon groves. They passed countless little villages of white granite houses with gray roofs—a few painted orange—neat and clean and with a sort of pattern to their random clusters. Some hugged the seashore while others perched atop the basalt cliffs as though a giant hand had set them there. She saw mules and mule carts, a few bicycles, and still fewer cars. Lisa noted the way narrow stone paths cut through the hills like so many white threads. There was an unyielding hardness to the stone face of this island that contrasted with the lushness of the palm trees and the tall cypresses, and the softness of the fig and date arbors.

It was late afternoon when they finally reached Cara- mania, and the taxi rolled slowly through the town which huddled at the edge of the sea. Chickens crossed their paths with total uncon- cern. A few old men looked up from the coffeehouses as they passed. They had just reached the end of the town when the taxi halted. Lisa looked out to see the big house rising up from the water's edge, towering and massive. She had never seen it before, not even a picture of it, yet, in some strange way, she knew it at once. This was Orion Hall, touching the water at one side and seeming to grow out of the hills on the other. It rose in a series of terraces. Set back from the terraces was the great castlelike house, two tall turrets standing at each end. The great house seemed to frown down on the little village, forbiddingly, omi- nously, possessively, the two big turrets coming down like the legs of a huge eagle. In between the two turret legs was the main body of the house, the top parapet curved outward, beaklike. It was a forbidding place and yet Lisa felt herself drawn to it, want- ing to rush inside.

She hurried along with Maggie and pushed against the tall oak door at the bottom of the house. The door opened slowly, just enough for them to enter, and Lisa was inside first. She was struck by the silence of the great house as she stood in awe and gazed around her. The walls were of huge stone blocks with dark oak paneling in the entranceway. Stone and tile floors and cor- ridors stretched out in all directions. Lisa walked to the edge of what was obviously the main dining hall. A huge, long table stood in the center, wrapped in protective sheets of cloth. A tremendous fireplace stood at the far end of the room, and on the walls crossed lances and various homed heads peered back at her.

She followed Maggie up a flight of steps and they found the bedrooms on the second floor, big rooms with a fireplace in each one. Maggie took the inside one and Lisa the other, diagonally across the arched corridor. Her windows looked out over the sea. Each room had a big, four-poster bed in it, also wrapped in protective sheets of cloth.

"We can undo things later," Maggie said. "It'll be dark soon. We'd best get some food and firewood in the house first. There's got to be some sort of market in town."

"I think I saw one down a sidestreet as we came in," Lisa said as they hurried down the stairs. Once again, despite the stone-walled, closed corridors and the grim massiveness of the place, it didn't seem a house that had been closed for over half a century. No, it seemed a house waiting for someone to return to it and she felt strangely drawn to Orion Hall once again. She wondered why, because it was really quite a frightening, forbidding place.

Outside, Lisa found the narrow street she had glimpsed before. The market was beyond it, opening up into a small square. There were stalls of fruits and vegetables, meats and sausages. There were mostly old women, very old women, tending the stalls, in long black dresses with black shawls pulled up over their heads, giving them all a nunlike appearance. There were few young women, Lisa noted, and the few she saw also wore somber clothes. But they had their heads bare and she envied the thick, luxuriously shining blackness of their hair. She and Maggie were, of course, new in town and she expected to be stared at, but not the way she saw the old women look at her—some with frowns of disbelief, some with their mouths open, some with what could only be called a fear in their black eyes. She had to think again of the strange way the man in the high black boots had looked at her outside the hotel in London. Maggie had halted at a stall where three black-shawled, wrinkled old crones stood. One of them looked at Lisa, crossed herself, and turned away. Suddenly another of them reached out and thrust a handful of fruit at the girl.

Lisa looked at the round, red-orange fruit about the size of a plum and felt herself shrinking away, her face contorting in unreasoned fear and horror, and she heard her voice gasping through tightened throat muscles. "No," she cried out. "No. Take them away." She recoiled in horror, turning her head.

"Lisa, what is it?" It was Maggie's voice and the older woman's hand on her arm. Lisa looked up. fearfully, and saw that the old woman had withdrawn the fruit. "What in heaven's name upset you so, child?" Maggie asked. "They're only pomegranates. Haven't you ever seen pomegranates before?"

Lisa shook her head and managed the one word "no."

"Well, there's no need to be so upset," the older woman frowned. "Why, you're trembling. What is it, my dear?"

"I don't know," Lisa said hoarsely. "I don't know."

"Come on, I'm finished here anyway," Maggie said, taking the girl's arm. "We'll go back to Orion Hall. I think you're just overtired."

Maggie took her purchases and swept off and Lisa followed, grateful to be hurrying away, aware of the stares of the village women. Her breath was returning to normal but she was still sick inside, absolutely unable to understand what had happened. Why had such horror and nausea flooded over her that way? That in itself was frightening, incomprehensible. She was glad to get inside the towering walls of Orion Hall, shutting out the village.

She helped Maggie unpack her purchases and then went outside to find some firewood. There were dry branches at the side of the house around the curved stones of one of the huge turrets and she brought in enough for both fireplaces, making several trips. They ate in Maggie's room before the fire and she felt herself unwind as she listened to Maggie's plans for the coming day. It helped to take her mind off the strange incident in the village. Not that she would forget it. She could still taste the horror that had seized her.

"We'll go to the mayor tomorrow and see about some servant help around the house," Maggie said, "even if it's only a man or an old couple. I'll need some help in getting the furniture and linens out of the storeroom or the cellar or wherever everything's been kept. It'll take months to put this place into any kind of shape but thank goodness it's not all dusty and cobwebby."

Lisa joined in the fun of planning and they talked until Maggie grew tired, and then the girl went down the hall and across to her room. She built a fire quickly. It was not a cold night but the old house held dampness and chill in its stones. She walked to the window and looked down at the terraces, the first one just outside, with a door opening onto it from the room. The second terrace was beyond it and the third one beyond that, rising up from the sea. She saw a line of stone steps at the back of the terraces leading down from one to the other. The moon, hanging high, was a cold, milk-white lantern tracing a pathway across the sea. Lisa put on a cardigan and went to the door that opened onto the terrace. The bolt was rusted shut and she tugged and pushed and pulled to no avail. She took a heavy andiron from before the fireplace and hammered on the bolt until it finally moved. A little more hammering and it slid back with a rusty groan. Lisa put down the andiron and pulled at the door. It swung open and she stepped down four stone steps to the terrace. She walked to the edge and looked down at the next two terraces, then back at the great stone turrets of Orion Hall faintly glistening in the night, their dark stones touched with the moonlight. Deciding to go down to the other terraces she turned and walked to the stone steps at the rear. She reached the big granite block at the top of the steps and turned to start down the narrow flight of stairs when she was suddenly seized by invisible hands that held her there, invisible chains that bound her legs to the top step. The same sudden, unexplainable dread that had seized her at the market square came to her again, this time with greater fear and a bone-chilling, icy coldness. She tried to move but her legs refused and she felt herself shrinking back, her body sliding itself against the stone side of the stairway wall. She heard the hard sound of her own breathing as she gazed down into the blackness of the stone steps, ominous, foreboding, frightening. She tried to force herself to move forward, to go down the steps, but something inside her was pulling her back, making her tremble, and she felt her body grow wet with sudden perspiration. She turned and found her legs running off with her, back into the house. Slamming the door shut behind her she fell onto the big bed and lay there until her body stopped quivering. Finally she rose, undressed, and got into bed beneath the heavy covering.

What was wrong with her, she wondered, frightened. What was happening to her? Was it merely the frightening ominousness of the steps as they disappeared into blackness? Somehow that was not enough, not for the icy dread that had seized her. Had her own dark imaginings made her react in strange ways to simple things? Why did this cavernous old house seem so frightening and so comfortable to her at the same time? She turned on her side, recalling Maggie's words about her dark and troubled imagination. She wouldn't let it gain the upper hand and hold her in its powers. She was just overtired, Lisa told herself, and finally she went to sleep, tossing and turning fitfully. She dreamed strange dreams in which black-robed figures slowly walked through mountainous waves like a line of underwater pallbearers. She woke up wet with perspiration and saw that the moonlight had flooded her room with its blue-white light. She went to the window and gazed down at the terraces and the sea below, at the beginning of the winding steps that went down at the rear of the flagstones. Finally she went back to bed and to sleep, aware in a dim way that unknown forces were gathering themselves in the towering, dark walls of Orion Hall.

CHAPTER THREE

*"Too lightly opened are a woman's ears; her
fence downtrod by many trespassers."*

—Aeschylus

Lisa woke and dressed in a white blouse and linen hip-huggers of bright orange, determined to forget the strange incidents of the past twenty-four hours. Maggie greeted her with the news that she had been up for over an hour and had found the storeroom filled with furniture and pewter flatware and all sorts of things waiting to be unpacked and unwrapped.

"But we'll need help," Maggie said. "Let's go into the village and see what we can get. When I sent my notice of residency to the mayor I mentioned I'd need some live-in help."

Lisa followed her aunt out into the hot glare of the sun and the sparklingly clear air. She looked up into the hillsides rising behind Orion Hall. The tangerine bushes were flashes of fire among the dark green of the olive trees. The village itself was slightly less indolent than it had been the day before, with more men delivering produce in two-wheeled, donkey carts. The mayor, a small, dour man in an ill-fitting dark blue suit, was in his office, a bare-walled room, and he was as uncommunicative as the place was barren. There was but one man available in Caramania, he told Maggie, an old, one-eyed man, something of a village outcast, by the name of Nikos.

"The people of Caramania are not interested in outsiders," the mayor said. "There are families here who have never been away from the village for five generations and none have ever been off Cyprus."

"Send this man to me," Maggie said, annoyance in her voice, with a note of contempt she did not try to hide. Maggie had never had any patience with foolish clannishness, an attitude Lisa shared. They went outside and Maggie turned to the girl.

"They'll change their time after I'm here a while," she said. "I'm going back to the house. I want to be there when the man arrives. Why don't you snoop around a bit on your own and learn about the village?"

"Good idea," Lisa said. "I'll buy some vegetables while I'm at it. I'll be back soon."

Lisa walked away, down the narrow village streets, past the old men at the coffeehouses, conscious of their glances, In her orange slacks and white blouse she was, compared to the somberly dressed women of the village, like the tangerines amid the olive trees, a flash of brilliance and boldness. She stepped aside to let a car go past slowly and smiled at the look of appreciation in the driver's eyes as he took in her long, lithe figure. She walked through the market square head held high, but once again she was conscious of the stares of the old crones. It wasn't the curiosity or the envy or even the faint hostility that bothered her. She could understand those things. It was the strange fearfulness in their dark eyes that baffled her and made her uneasy. Suddenly she was desperately hoping no one would thrust a cluster of pomegranates at her again and she recalled the inexplicable incident of yesterday with new fright. Forcing herself, she stopped at one of the market stalls and bought celery, radishes, ripe black olives, and collards. Arms laden with her purchases she turned and escaped from the square, her head bent low. She rounded the comer and almost ran into an old man wheeling a bicycle with one hand while carrying another strapped to his back. Instantly an idea occurred to her. A bicycle would be the perfect thing for getting around the island, even though it might be a little hilly for ideal riding. She spoke to the old man in her best Greek, which surprised him. She had some trouble with the Greek word for bicycle, which she didn't know, but she managed to get across the idea that she wanted to purchase one of his cycles. He refused vigorously, saying he needed them both, one to ride and one for spare parts. She was about to turn away in disappointment when she heard a voice at her side.

"Perhaps I can help the *signorina,*" the voice said, in English, with just the faintest touch of a Greek accent. Lisa turned to look up at the man standing beside her and her voice caught in her throat. For a long moment it was as if the pages of history had riffled backwards and she stood before an ancient Greek statue come to life in all its vibrant beauty. The man before her wore only slacks and a towel draped across his chest, still glistening wet from the waters of the sea. Tall, with curly black hair and eyes of deep, liquid brown, he looked down at her with his full, sensuous lips smiling easily. His tanned skin rippled across a broad, beautifully muscled chest. Truly she had never seen a more handsome man in her life. She saw him throwing the discus in ancient Thrace, marching beside Hannibal, debating amid the columns of the Acropolis. He was all she'd ever studied and read of ancient Greek beauty come to life, standing before her in flesh and blood. It was little wonder that it took a long moment for her to find her tongue.

"I am Demetrius," he said simply, his smile widening into dazzling sunlight. "The gods smile on me today. I was wondering how I might meet you. I saw you yesterday when you arrived with the other lady."

"My aunt," Lisa said. "I'm Lisa Bowen."

His smile flashed again to wrap itself around her like a warming garland. "Well, Lisa, there is no need to haggle with that old man when I can get you a bicycle easily. And at a better price than he would ask."

"Do you sell bicycles?" Lisa asked, hoping he wouldn't really be in anything so prosaic as that. She was happily relieved when he shook his head.

"No, but I've many friends who have cycles they do not use," he answered. "I am a courier for the Greek government and I travel among the islands. But Caramania is my favorite spot and I spend most of my time here."

"It's beautiful here," Lisa said. "What I've seen of it. Though I don't think we're too welcome."

"You have come to open Orion Hall, I understand," he said, taking her packages from her. She didn't protest. "News travels fast on Cyprus. But you must forgive these simple people. They hold their little world close to them. They fear the outside. They fear tomorrow and prefer to live in the past."

He fell into step beside her and she turned toward the main street. His deep brown eyes danced with a warm fire that reached out to her. "You have much to learn of life here," he said lightly. "Tonight there is to be a happy time in the square, a joyful occasion, what we call a *panigyri*. I would like to take you and show you the people enjoying themselves. Suppose I bring you the bicycle and then we could go down to the festivities. I would be terribly honored."

"That sounds wonderful," Lisa said, trying to hold her enthusiasm to reasonable proportions. Her smile matched his and there was no hesitation now. "How about eight o'clock?"

"I will be there," he said. "I must motor to Famagusta but I'll be back in plenty of time."

He bowed, a short, quick bow, and pressed her hand. She took back her packages and watched him walk off, a lithe grace in his every step, and she now knew why the ancient Greeks worshiped male beauty even more than female. "Demetrius," Lisa said softly. Even the name was beautiful. She had intended to return to Orion Hall but instead she decided to walk up the winding path into the hills that were suddenly less grim. It had turned into a wonderful, wonderful day and it promised to get even better. She walked the slow, gentle rise of the little road that cut back upon itself and twisted its way upwards with delightful unexpectedness. She paused every so often to gaze down at the blue Mediterranean and the white houses of Caramania below. At the far end of the village, almost obscured by the rows of olive trees on the hillside, she saw the towering turrets of Orion Hall. Turning, she walked on, her packages not the least bit heavy.

Lisa had just reached a sharp right-angle bend in the narrow road when she heard an oath followed by the sharp cry of a girl's voice and then the sound of a blow. She hurried around the bend and her eyes first saw the girl lying in the road, white blouse and dark green skirt covering a young, ripe figure. Her face was darkly beautiful with long, flowing hair, but her eyes were those of a hurt deer. Then she saw the man, those cavernous eyes, the piercing fierce glare, and she almost gasped. But the girl looked up at her in a silent plea for help and Lisa felt her temper explode at this crag-faced man who had haunted her ever since she arrived in London. He had one arm raised to strike the girl again and held it in that threatening position.

"Don't you dare," Lisa shot out, letting her packages slip to the ground. She hadn't thought of how she could possibly stop this giant in his high black boots but that didn't matter. She knew from past experience that little ever did when her temper exploded.

"What gives you the right to strike her?" Lisa asked, fire in her own brown eyes. "Who are you anyway?"

The man stepped back and lowered his arm. "It is not enough you come here," he said through gritted teeth. "You make trouble, too. You will pay, too. Just like she did."

He turned and for the first time Lisa saw the small, two wheeled, hand-drawn cart of cloth and skins behind him. He pushed it viciously, almost running over the girl on the road. As he strode off with the cart, he spat at her and she turned her face aside. Lisa, frowning, was still turning his strange words over in her mind but she could make no sensible meaning out of them. The girl pulled herself to her feet and turned to Lisa.

"It is over now," she said quietly. "I was bonded to work for him five years ago and to marry him someday. It was arranged that way but now it is done with."

"Arranged that way?" Lisa exclaimed. "In this day and age?"

"Here on Cyprus things are done in the old ways," the girl said. "But I accepted help from you, an outsider. I cannot go back again."

"I shouldn't think you'd want to," Lisa huffed. "You can come work for my aunt and live in Orion Hall." She saw the girl pause and then shrug.

"Why not?" she said wryly. "I am not one of them anyway. I was brought here from Crete as a little girl. I will go with you. My name is Thera."

"All right, Thera," Lisa said. "Let's get to the house and tell Maggie. That's your new boss."

"There is a shortcut through the hills and the olive grove," Thera said. "It will bring us out alongside the big house. Come, I will show you."

Lisa followed, and the girl led her through a narrow, steep pathway, hardly more than a trail. "Who is that man?" Lisa asked as they paused for breath at one point. "What does he do here?"

"His name is Kosta Danapoulis," Thera replied. "Kosta is all he is called and he does many things. Sometimes he fishes on the fishing boats. Sometimes he travels to other places for a man who pays him to deliver things. Of late he has made many trips but he never spoke to me of his work."

Lisa felt her lips tighten. So the man, Kosta, may have been in London on business of his own. Maybe it had all been coincidental and she had let her imagination run away with her. Maybe. But that didn't explain the terrible way he had stared at her. Nor his cryptic words. Thera turned and started off and Lisa put her thoughts aside to clamber after the girl. They emerged alongside the east turret of Orion Hall and a few steep steps down brought them to the main door. When Maggie heard she had returned with a girl to live in and work, she was more than delighted. Thera spoke English, too, a double stroke of good fortune. The old, one-eyed man, Nikos, was already busy pulling things from the storeroom and Lisa translated a few instructions from Maggie to him. Later, over dinner, she told Maggie about Demetrius and the older woman's eyes twinkled. "Wonderful," she exclaimed. "Nothing like a handsome man to make things come alive, is there?"

Lisa laughed, glanced at her watch, and hurried upstairs to change. As she dressed she thought again of Thera and the man, Kosta, and of his strange words. *You will pay, too. Just like she did.* Who else had paid? And for what? Who was "she?" She hadn't said anything to Maggie about the man's mysterious words, just as she hadn't mentioned the strange incident at the terrace steps last night. It didn't seem that important anymore. It was passed, to be forgotten. She slipped on an iridescent blue dress and looked shimmeringly delicious, the low, round neckline revealing the cream-white swell of her full breasts. She was glad she'd gotten ready early because Demetrius arrived only a few moments later, carrying the bicycle. A cream jacket and a black turtleneck shirt made his straight-nosed Grecian handsomeness that much stronger. She insisted on paying him for the bicycle and he didn't try to embarrass her by refusing. Maggie appeared as they were about to leave and whispered in Lisa's ear.

"God, he's handsome, all right," she said. "I never trust men that handsome. It's a thing with me."

"Not with me," Lisa laughed. "I don't mind it a bit." She took Demetrius' arm and they went out the door.

The *panigyri* was held in a square at the edge of the stone quay, close by the cooling water of the sea. There were more younger women than she'd seen in town and they wore brighter but simple clothes. An old man with a concertina and two bouzouki players furnished the music. With Demetrius by her side Lisa sensed greater acceptance by the others. Or maybe she just didn't give a damn, she told herself with characteristic realism. Demetrius was more than enough to make any girl's evening. She could feel the sensuous warmth of the man radiate an almost animal charm. He introduced her to Greek folk dances, guiding her body with a light but firm hold on her waist that sent positively improper thrills through her. Finally they sat down to the dinner, suckling pig sizzling over a charcoal fire, stewed lamb and shish kebab, stuffed tomatoes and sliced cucumbers, steaming pots of rice and eggplant, tender morsels of lamb wrapped in olive leaves. It was a feast of memorable taste and proportions, and like the others, Lisa drank deeply and often of the *retsina,* an aromatic red wine highly flavored in the making with the essences of spices, peppers, cloves, and aromatic gums. Ordinarily it would have been too pungent for Lisa but it seemed just right to cut the richness of the foods. Cyprus was certainly a lovely place and Caramania a lovely village by the time the night grew late and the dancing and feasting ended. The *panigyri,* the time for wiping away ordinary cares, was over. They walked slowly back to the towering house and it was then that she told Demetrius of her meeting with Thera and the man, Kosta, after she had left him that morning.

"You should not have interfered," Demetrius said, his face serious.

"I'd do it again," she snapped, surprised at her own vehemence. "I don't believe in going along with stupidity and wrong just because it's traditional."

"Wrong," Demetrius sighed and Lisa's eyes traveled over the sculptured beauty of his face. "What is wrong to you, with your background and heritage, may be perfectly right to someone with another background."

Lisa reflected for a moment. "I'll have to think more about that," she said. "And I've had too much wine to think much tonight."

They had reached the heavy oaken door of Orion Hall and the moon was a soft glow with clouds beginning to form over it. "You are a really beautiful girl," Demetrius said, his hand touching her hair lightly, running gently down the back of her neck where she had her hair swept up. She felt the warmth of his fingers on her neck.

"Perhaps we could see each other after your brief stay here in Caramania," he suggested. "I would try to arrange for that to be possible."

"Maybe my stay here won't be brief," she said.

"I see," Demetrius said, and for a moment she thought there was a sudden hardness in his voice. But it was only imagined, she was sure, as his lips suddenly closed on hers. "So much the better," he said. His hand on the small of her back pressed her against him and she felt the surge of desire flood over her and her lips parted to answer his. But finally she pulled away. She knew the strength of her own desires and it was something she guarded against. There was such a thing as too much too quickly. Besides, this Greek god of a man was too power-fill to take chances with. If she decided to give more of herself to him it would be that much greater for the waiting.

"May I see you again tomorrow?" Demetrius asked with that old-world charm that was part of him.

"I'll probably have a lot to do to help Maggie around the house tomorrow," she answered. "Why don't we make it the next day."

"Fine," he smiled. "We will go on a picnic. I'll show you another part of the hills of Cyprus."

He turned and walked off and Lisa watched him go, moving easily with a swinging grace that was sensuous in itself. She closed the door and stood for a moment in the silence of the big house. Kerosene lamps had been put into wall brackets, she saw, their flames casting eerie shadows on the stone walls. She hurried to her room and into bed. The wine was still with her and she felt as warm and contented as a cat by a fire. Demetrius had changed the island of Cyprus for her with one smile. Dimly she wondered if it were because she so desperately wanted to turn away from the strange things that had happened. No matter, she told herself sleepily, content to accept it if it were so. Demetrius made a lovely hiding place.

She slept quickly and soundly and it was in the early pre-dawn hours that she woke to sit upright in the big bed, wondering why she had wakened. Then she heard it, a half-singing, half-wailing sound coming from outside. Swinging out of bed she rushed to the window and tried to peer down to the terraces but a wispy, trailing fog shifted and cloaked the night. Something white, like a sail, seemed to move in the water beneath the bottom terrace just as the fog closed in to obstruct her view. The wailing singing began again and then died away and she thought she saw a dark shape on the bottom terrace, by the wall. She pressed her face against the window but the vaporous fog drew a trail across the terrace and blotted out the image. She stood there waiting for it to part. When it did she saw nothing but the empty terrace and the sea beyond it, equally empty. The fog blew itself away before her eyes and she stared out at the terraces. Something had been down there. She was sure of it. She shivered and went back to the bed. Was she really sure of it, she asked herself. Night shadows can play tricks and wine lingers to tease the eyes. She turned on her side and went back to sleep, letting thoughts of Demetrius Warm the chill of her body. Not until the morning sun laid its warm fingers across her face did she waken again.

CHAPTER FOUR

"Things are not always what they seem."
—Phaedrus

Aｆｔｅｒ ｂｒｅａｋｆａｓｔ Maggie had Lisa stay with the old man, Nikos, until she was certain he knew what she wanted him to do during the morning. Thera was set about scrubbing and waxing the big pieces of furniture that had been pulled from the storeroom yesterday. The old man worked cheerfully enough under Lisa's direction though she caught him studying her from time to time, a small frown on his wrinkled face. When she met his eyes he would quickly look away and return to his work. It was past midmorning before Lisa got a chance to slip out onto the terrace, once again going through the doorway from her room. She looked down at the third terrace below where she had seen the strange shape in the fog. She wanted to go down to that terrace, to walk upon it herself and examine the flagstones. Turning briskly, she walked toward the head of the stone steps at the rear of the terrace. As she neared the big granite stone at the top of the steps, her heart began to beat wildly and she grew angrily impatient with herself. But a touch of anxiety *was* to be expected after what had happened the other night. She rounded the big stone, paused at the top of the steps, and felt her body begin to tremble. Her hands had turned ice cold and her breasts heaved with the deep harshness of her breathing. The steps stretched down in front of her, ordinary stone steps in the bright sunlight. She tried to move forward and felt her legs stiffen, her stomach harden into a knot, and suddenly a wave of absolute fear swept over her, fear so real and so terrible she became nauseated. She shrank back against the stones of the wall, trembling so violently now she almost fell. Cringing there, unable to stop the sick nausea in the pit of her stomach or her body's terrible shaking, she flung herself backwards, away from the steps. She fell against the big white stone and clung to it, her hands almost as white as the granite as they clutched its unyielding surface. She stayed there until the nausea passed and her body halted its trembling.

"This is absolutely asinine," she said aloud, her voice a hoarse whisper. "It must be some crazy kind of mental block." She straightened up, her eyes wide, unable to cope with or really comprehend the strange occurrence. Yet the explanation of a mental block was the only reasonable one. That first night she'd been overtired, on edge, and the steps had been black and ominous and frightening. Perhaps that night had set up some crazy, unreasonable psychic reaction still inside her. She walked across the terrace clutching at the explanation while wondering why she was so dissatisfied with it. And now, even more, she wanted to go down to see that lowest terrace. The strange incidents at the steps made it seem as if some invisible force were acting to keep her from doing so and Lisa felt her stubbornness rising immediately. She looked up at the sloping hillside that stretched beyond the wall of the terrace. She could go down it and would most certainly come out at the bottom beside the sea. Surely there would be some sort of shore path past the seawall of the terrace that would lead her to the front of it and steps to take her up to it.

Lisa stepped onto a small stone bench, caught hold of a tree branch, and swung herself over the wall and onto the hillside. She had put on a light green blouse and a green miniskirt and she was glad for the freedom of movement it gave her. The hill was steeper than she'd imagined and a tight skirt would have made passage impossible. She followed a small trail, making her way through a field of wild anemones, clusters of tough hillside scrub brush, and a field of pine trees. She paused to rest and peer down at the sea.

Orion Hall was hardly visible now as the trail led her sideways as well as down, but she didn't care about that. She wanted to see the land on this side of the great house and she glimpsed what seemed like a sharp point that jutted out into the water a few hundred yards beyond, the comer of the seawall. Getting to her feet, she started down again and suddenly the line of trees ended and she could see a small cottage below her, set back from the water's edge. It had the usual gray slate roof but the walls had been painted fight blue. If she could get down to it, she could walk back along the shoreline to Orion Hall as she'd planned. Focusing on the cottage as a guide, she was climbing down diagonally toward it when suddenly the slope turned into an almost straight drop. Some fifty yards further down she saw it bulge out again in a more gradual incline of tall grass. Turning, she dug one foot into the soft soil and seized one of the scrub bushes with her two hands. Carefully she lowered herself down the steep drop.

Lisa felt rather than heard the brush tear loose from the soil. She grabbed out desperately, trying to catch hold of another piece of brush, but there was none and she felt herself falling. She dug her fingers into the earth to slow her fall and it stopped her from going over backwards but she was sliding, tumbling down now, her momentum increasing. She felt the pain of small stones digging into her back as she bounced off the slope and her skirt billowed up as her legs hit the edge of a small protrusion and bounced off it. She was tumbling head over heels as she hit the slope at the point where it leveled off. But her body had gathered its own momentum and she couldn't stop herself. The tall grasses tore off in her hands as she grasped at them and then suddenly she felt herself caught, felt her wild tumbling stop as she was held fast against the ground. She looked up to see blue eyes set in a pleasant face topped by a shock of reddish hair. The man had hold of her arms, pinning them down against the ground, and now he let go and pulled her up to a sitting position. His blue eyes held hers with a cool amusement.

"Epharisto!" Lisa said automatically. "Thank you."

The eyes had been smiling coolly at her right along. Now the face joined them.

"My pleasure," the man said in English that held the faint touch of a Celtic burr. "It was worth seeing. You have damn beautiful legs."

Lisa pulled at her skirt, not that it went down very far.

"If you were coming down to see me, I can tell you an easier way," he said affably.

"I wasn't coming down to see you," Lisa said. "I take it that's your cottage down there."

He nodded and leaned back on one elbow. He had a way of keeping a quiet, impassive face while his eyes held a sardonic gleam of assured self-confidence. He was good-looking, she decided, in a quiet sort of way. Nothing like the shattering handsomeness of Demetrius, though.

"I'm Michael Barry," he said. "And you're the girl with the woman who's come to live at Orion Hall."

"News does travel here," Lisa commented. "Yes. I'm Lisa Bowen." His eyes were studying her with a cool amusement that she found slightly irritating. As he wasn't a Greek or a Cypriote, she wondered what he did here on the island. He wore a faded denim shirt and she noted a small ax and a chisel stuck in his belt.

"You are living here on Cyprus?" she tossed out. "Or just tourist vacationing?"

"I'm an archaeologist," Michael Barry said. "I've been living here for over a year now. Cyprus is a heaven for archaeologists. Do you know anything about the island?"

"Not really," Lisa said. "But I do want to learn about it."

He sat up straighter and held her gaze for a moment, his eyes still dancing with that reserved, private amusement. He pointed to the wide expanse of hillside and sea that stretched before them.

"Behold a storehouse of history," he said. "Cyprus is a living page of history, a place where contrasting cultures paused to leave their mark. Today it is primarily Greek, but not Greek such as Athens. It carries the flavor of the Levant, and even the Greek Cypriote is a man unto himself."

"It does seem to be a land of contrasts," Lisa said "Even the people are full of contrasts. They are handsome and sensuous and stem and dour."

"That's the inward direction of the Greek character," he laughed. "Someone once said that the Greek character is like the moon. Light on one side, black on the other. But Cyprus itself has been the watering place for the conquerors of history. Those advancing on the eastern lands used Cyprus as their base. The armies of Alexander the Great, Augustus, Richard the Lion-Hearted, and Saint Louis all paused here at Cyprus. Those bursting from the east to conquer the west first came to Cyprus. Ptolemy exhorted his Egyptians here. Cyrus, Haroun-al-Raschid, Hannibal—all stopped here. On Cyprus you have Arab mosques and Christian monasteries left by the forces of history to mark their passing."

He stopped abruptly, his blue eyes twinkling at her as if in apology for his momentary seriousness. "Did you know that Anthony gave Cyprus to Cleopatra as a present?" he laughed.

The sun sent copper shafts glinting through his reddish hair as he unabashedly looked up and down her body, taking in her beauty.

"Sorry I can't match Anthony, but maybe I can give you some further help," he grinned. "Where were you going in such an unplanned fashion just now?"

"Down to the bottom of the hill, to the shore," she said. "I want to walk back to Orion Hall along the shore and see the bottom terrace from the seawall. I haven't really seen it except from the window of my room."

Suddenly she was afraid he might ask her why she didn't simply go down the terrace steps. But he didn't. Instead he smiled a slow, wise smile while his eyes danced at her.

"Ah, the last terrace by the seawall," he intoned. "Where Athena still prowls the night when the fog hides the moon, waiting for her vengeance. Or so the villagers believe."

"Athena?" Lisa said, suddenly all alert and tense. "The last Mistress of Orion Hall?"

"Yes," he said. "Do you know the legend?"

"No," Lisa said. "I'd heard there were all sorts of legends."

"And some more than legend," he said. "The people of Caramania still believe that Athena prowls the terrace at Orion Hall, or certainly her spirit. Of late there has been a renewal of their fears, a reawakening of the legend, I hear."

"Why do they believe that she still prowls the terrace?"

"Oh, that's a long story and part of history. Reality and legend are often quite closely connected, you know."

Lisa felt the dryness in the back of her throat as she thought about the dark shadows and sounds she had seen and heard in the fogbound night. "Surely you don't believe in spirits prowling about old terraces?" she cast out. Michael Barry turned a bright grin on her that was transparently noncommittal.

"I believe in everything and in nothing," he said. "In archaeology we are always finding things that make legends real and
reality legendary."

"Will you tell me the legend of Athena?" Lisa asked. "She was
my great-grandmother."

"I suspected something like that," Michael said as he reached
out one hand and deftly opened the clip that held her hair up
in a semi-ponytail. "Fantastic," he muttered as her hair fell
down loosely to her shoulders. His eyes roamed over her. "Quite
fantastic."

"Am I supposed to say thank you or something on that order?"
Lisa said, feeling her annoyance rising with this self-assured man
whose eyes constantly held veiled laughter.

"No, I wasn't commenting on your good looks," he grinned
at her. "Have you been down to the cellar of Orion Hall yet?"

"No," she said, her eyes questioning.

"I suggest you go down and have a look about," he said
cheerfully.

"Have you been there?" she asked, annoyed. He nodded
affably and she felt her irritation rising.

"Isn't that a bit presumptuous?" she said curtly. "After all, it
is private property."

"Nobody had lived there for over half a century," he said, not
the slightest bit bothered by her annoyance. "I suppose it's presumptuous to go around digging up people's graves and temples,
too. But we archaeologists do it all the time. Occupational dis-
ease, snooping."

"Tell me the legend of Athena," Lisa persisted.

"Have a look down in the cellar first, Lisa my girl," Michael
Barry said, dismissing her request with a wide grin. He got up
suddenly and reached down, pulling her to her feet.

"Thanks a lot," she said, sarcasm dripping from her voice.

"Anytime," he said cheerfully, unflustered, his eyes mocking, laughing. He could certainly use some of Demetrius' old-world charm and sincerity, she told herself silently. He started down the hillside, holding his hand out for her to take. She refused, but after she'd fallen twice she decided it would be better to take it than see the silent laughter in his eyes. His arms were strong and swung her lightly over the steep spots and soon they were at his little cottage, the sea only a handful of yards away.

"Care to come in?" he asked casually, making the question completely noncommittal.

"Will you tell me the story of Athena?" she asked, eyeing him shrewdly. She could play games, too.

"Some time," he smiled.

"Thank you for helping me up on the hill," she said, unable to hide her temper, the small smile edging his lips making her angrier. He continued to regard her with that mocking look and she turned abruptly and walked away. She didn't see the amused light go out of his eyes and his face grow suddenly thoughtful as he watched her go off. She walked briskly and saw that she had indeed gone beyond a point of land that jutted out into the sea, cutting off a view of Orion Hall. Only when she rounded the point did she see the great house towering up on the hillside, reaching its stone walls down to the sea. She paused at the point for a moment to look back at the little cottage. Michael Barry had gone inside and she had a moment's regret she hadn't taken his invitation. But that was only curiosity, she knew. Besides, he knew the legend and history of Athena and she meant to get it from him if she couldn't learn it elsewhere. She was sure she'd be seeing him again.

The shoreline grew narrower as she neared the seawall that came down straight from the lowest terrace, and when she reached the wall she found only a narrow ledge of stone between herself and the water. She could see that the water here was no sloping shoreline but deep right to the seawall. She inched herself along the ledge carefully. Not that she was afraid of falling in. She was an excellent swimmer; she just didn't relish an impromptu dip at the moment. Finally reaching the end of the stone ledge she stepped down onto soil again and the shoreline widened at once. She moved around to the side and saw the flight of steps leading up to the terrace. From where she stood she could see that the terrace was empty and she decided against trying to mount the short flight of steps. She had learned what she had come to learn, that there was a flight of steps leading up to the lowest terrace as well as those leading down to it from above. Following the outside of the house, she walked upwards away from the water, passing through a cluster of short pine bushes, and found herself at the front door.

Inside the house Thera was setting up pewter plates on the big, dark, wood bureau that had been put into the main dining hall. Maggie was upstairs taking a nap. It seemed a good idea, for the afternoon sun had grown very warm, but Lisa had other things on her mind. Thera didn't know where the cellar was and Lisa was sorry she hadn't asked Michael Barry. Once again she felt annoyance at his snooping around inside the great house. Three hall doors turned up false leads and she went into the big kitchen. One door there led her into a huge pantry. Then she saw the arched doorway at the far end of the room. Pulling the door open she saw the curved flight of stone steps leading down. Returning briefly to Thera, she got one of the kerosene lamps that had been unearthed from the storage room. The lamp held in one hand, Lisa went down the steps into the basement, the light casting flickering shadows in the huge, dank, damp, and clammy cellar.

There was more furniture piled in careless profusion here, and boxes and rusted tools and frayed bundles of drapery. She moved through the jumble of dusty objects and was beginning to wonder why Michael Barry had suggested she come down here when the lamplight reached out to reveal a big canvas in a heavy gold frame standing against the wall, a sheet draped over it. The face of the painting was turned to the wall and Lisa put the kerosene lamp down on top of a wooden crate and began to pull at the painting. It was as tall as she and heavy and she tugged at it until it was far enough from the wall to be swung around. She turned the painting, propped it up against the crate, and pulled the sheet from it. In the silence of the cellar she heard the sound of her own breath being drawn in sharply. She stared at the full length portrait on the canvas. Except for the clothes, she might almost have been staring into a mirror. The young woman who looked out at her from the canvas was almost a twin, her thin, straight nose, soft lips, and wide cheekbones just like her own. Her figure, in a long white gown with a black cape thrown back, was long-waisted and narrow-hipped, identical to the contours of Lisa's own body. The girl's hair fell loosely down to her shoulders in exactly the same way as Lisa's hair now hung. Only the eyes were different. The eyes in the painting were deeper, more piercing, with a dark intensity. But the likeness was startling enough and Lisa, transfixed before the painting, thought of the old women in the village and of the man, Kosta. Now she knew why they stared at her. Some of the oldest ones might have remembered Athena, Mistress of Orion Hall. The others obviously knew this portrait, or in other ways knew what she had looked like. And it was Athena—the single name attached to the frame at the bottom wasn't even necessary for Lisa.

The girl pulled the sheet back over the uncanny likeness and left the cellar.

Upstairs the house was quiet and Maggie was still napping. Lisa marched out of the house, along the side, through the pine bushes, and down to the water's edge. Damn that Michael Barry, she said to herself. He had learned things in his dusty old snooping and he knew more than he'd revealed. She intended to find out what it was. Maybe it would provide a rational explanation for the strange things that had beset her here in this old house. Once again she edged her way along the narrow ledge of the seawall until she reached the other end and stepped down onto the hard-grained sand of the shoreline. The portrait had not only shaken her with its frightening likeness but had brought back the rush of things she had held to one side: the incident with the pomegranates, her inability to go down the terrace steps, the strangely warm feeling she had for the ominous, forbidding monster of a house that was Orion Hall. What did these things mean? What could they mean? As she walked around the point of land, she felt a sudden chill pass through her body and once more knew that there were things here at Orion Hall that surpassed her understanding. Yet she insistently told herself that there had to be a logical explanation somewhere and she vowed to find it. Michael Barry and whatever he knew of the past would be as good a place to start as any.

But when she reached the little cottage, she found the door closed and a note tacked to it. "Out snooping" was all it said. "Damn!" Lisa muttered angrily. He could be gone till nightfall. She couldn't see Orion Hall around the point of land but a road stretched from the other side of the cottage, winding up into the hillside in a slow curve. Deciding that there was probably another hill route back to the village, she started up the road. This island of Cyprus was full of roads that cut back on each other. She walked on, soon out of sight of the cottage, and the road turned inward in a long, leisurely circle, cutting across the top of the hill. It would, she saw, eventually bring her back to the village, probably from the other side. She was striding along a flat section on the top of the hill when she saw the man approaching, pulling the two-wheeled cart. It was Kosta and she forced herself not to flinch. She saw the anger and hate in his eyes as she strode past, head held high. Was the hatred because she had defended Thera against him or was something more behind it? The question stayed with her as she walked on but, like so many other thoughts in her head, it went unanswered. How can there be answers, she wondered, when the questions themselves are riddles?

The sun was sinking and the Mediterranean turning a deep blue-violet as she neared Caramania, the road suddenly making a sharp turn and dipping down. She had guessed right for the road did bring her out on the far side of the village and she walked quickly through streets mostly deserted as the supper hour neared. Her legs were tired and she decided that the next time she'd use the bicycle Demetrius had brought her. Maggie was helping Thera fix dinner and they dined formally in the huge hall, looking terribly lost in its cavernous space but nonetheless enjoying the feel of it.

"Isn't this place going to be just too big for you, Maggie?" Lisa asked. "It's not as if you were in London where you had a lot of friends to invite to parties."

"It is too big but I'll have to make the best of it," Maggie answered. "And perhaps in time I'll make new friends here and put some life and laughter back into this old place."

Once again Lisa wondered why Maggie would "have to make the best of it," and she thought of what Maggie had said about being glad to be "settled and secure." But she didn't press the subject. She didn't say anything about the portrait, either. No doubt Maggie would discover it in time and see it as just a remarkable likeness. There was nothing that unusual about looking like an ancestor, Lisa knew, and to tell Maggie of the incidents at the terrace steps would gain her nothing. She had concluded that Maggie was strictly a realist and put little store in unexplained imaginings or emotional excursions. It was ironic in a way, Lisa mused, because she, too, had always been a realist, except insofar as her romantic nature went. In all other things she'd always been thought of as level-headed and not given to hysterics. Yet since she had come to Cyprus, to Orion Hall and this little village, she'd been far from level-headed.

The night had turned chilly but they decided against lighting the fire in the dining hall. "I'm going up to bed," Maggie announced. "All this work is hard on old bones when they're not used to it."

Lisa kissed her aunt on the cheek and watched the woman go up to her room. She waited a while, sipping the strong coffee Thera had made, and then decided to go to bed, too. Her legs were tired from all the walking she'd done. And she would be up early in the morning for her date with Demetrius and the picnic he'd promised her. In her room she made a fire and watched the wood blaze in the fireplace as she went to bed and stretched out in the warmth of the covers. She had put on a light shortie nightgown and smiled idly as she wondered if the girl in the painting in the cellar really did have as good a figure as she. Those long gowns and capes covered a multitude of sins, she wagered. The warmth of the fire reached out to caress her into sleep and it burned low, down to glowing embers, as the girl slept soundly. Hours had passed when suddenly she woke, her eyes snapping open in the dark. She lay there, listening, and then she heard the sound—soft singing that was not really singing and not really wailing but a strange, undulating sound of its own. She got out of bed and stepped to the terrace window. This time the fog had come in thickly, swirling and rolling across the terrace, turning the night into a thick, opaque wall. As her eyes tried to pierce the darkness, a bank of fog rolled aside and she glimpsed the lower terrace and a figure down there pacing in a long, black cape. Lisa felt her body grow cold as she peered down. The fog closed in over the figure and then lifted again. Someone was there, unmistakably there, beside the terrace wall. She saw the figure move down to the steps and then back again, pacing impatiently.

Her face grim, Lisa pulled on her blouse, threw a sweater over it, and wrapped a skirt around her waist as she flung open the terrace door. Moving through the fog, she made her way to the terrace steps. They would take her down to the figure on the last terrace without being seen, but even as she reached them, she knew she could not go down. Her skin began to crawl and the hard knot formed in her stomach as something pulled her back and made her cringe. She wouldn't waste time trying to fight down the strange psychic block, she decided. Instead she turned, ran back into the house and down the stairs to the front door. She would go to the bottom of the terrace, the way she had done this afternoon. In the fog she fell against the pine bushes but impatiently pushed her way through them, ignoring the stabs of pain. The fog down by the water was heavy and she groped her way, holding one hand against the outer wall of the house, suddenly stopping as she heard the sound of the sea. She was at the bottom of the terrace and the short flight of steps had to be near. The singing started in again, startlingly loud now, and its eerie wailing sound reached inside her and made her very heart cold. Her hands were wet with perspiration and she wiped them against her skirt. Using her hands, she moved along the wall, feeling for an edge of stone that would tell her she had found the steps leading up to the terrace. Suddenly a wisp of wind blew and the fog shredded for a moment. The steps were directly in front of her and there, on the top one, wreathed in dark mist, was the figure, black-robed, shadowy. The fog closed around it, then parted again, and the figure was still there. Who are you? Lisa wanted to shout but she found her voice had deserted her. She heard a movement, turned her head to peer through the fog that cloaked her, and then looked back up to the terrace. The figure was not there and Lisa moved forward, frowning. She heard another faint noise behind her, started to turn, and suddenly her head exploded with the pain of a vicious blow. She fell forward, stumbling, went to her knees while her head whirled and spun, and suddenly felt terribly light and about to fall off. Somehow she got to her feet, tried to run, and slammed into the wall of the house. The collision sent her reeling backwards, or had something else pitched her back? She didn't know. Everything was fading away and she was falling. The coldness of the water jarred her mind for a moment and the whirling stopped and she realized she had fallen into the sea. But the inky curtain that was both light and heavy all at the same time descended upon her again as she felt herself being swept out by the water. She tried to move her arms and legs but they refused to obey her feeble commands. Only the shock of the water had held off the curtain of unconsciousness, she realized, and instinctively she had breathed through her nose and kept her mouth closed. But her head hurt so and the black curtain was descending now, a welcome, sweet call to sleep. And yet, that small part of her mind still conscious told her that it would be the sleep of death. The curtain lowered further and she was suddenly so terribly tired and sleep so appealing. But an inner voice called to her in desperation. Float, it cried out, float. The command, torn from the primordial urge to survive, probed its way through her nearly unconscious mind. She moved her body in the water, turning on her back, aware of the heavy wetness of her clothes. The sea swept her along as she floated, fighting to stay awake. Float and stay conscious, the voice cried out again, and she obeyed with all her remaining willpower, shifting her body on the sea, feeling the water seize her in its soft grip to hold her afloat. The sweet curtain still beckoned but the girl fought back, clinging to consciousness, concentrating all her efforts on staying afloat and awake. The call to sleep grew less strong and she felt her mind clearing. She opened her eyes and saw the fog blanket around her, not so thick now, trailing vapors like long, pink-gray scarves in the wind. Her arms and legs were still weak and her head hurt but she was fully awake now and she let herself float on, gathering her strength meanwhile. Finally she turned over and began to swim but each stroke robbed her of precious energy, each movement of her arms was a tremendous effort.

Suddenly she saw a yellow, diffused light, not more than a hazy patch in the dark, vaporous fog. She swam toward it and it became larger as a strand of fog lifted and she could see the shore with the little cottage set back from the water's edge. She had been carried around the point by the tide and had been on her way to being swept out to sea. The brief glimpse of Michael Barry's cottage faded away as the fog closed in again and she renewed her strokes toward the diffused glare. But she felt her strength going fast, her water-soaked clothes dead weights on her arms and legs. She turned on her back to rest a while but realized she was being swept out to sea, losing whatever distance she had come toward shore. She turned over again and began to swim. The haze of light was her own beacon, her lighthouse of life, and she swam toward it with mounting desperation. Her body was draining of what little strength she had left and she felt herself go under. Struggling she pulled herself to the surface and screamed. The fog continued to swirl in front of her and she called out again, unable to judge how close she was to shore. The light wavered and was joined by another light, sharper and whiter, and she felt rather than saw the beam flash across her. She tried to tread water but only succeeded in thrashing frantically and her cry was weak as she went under again. Then strong hands found her and dragged her forward and she felt the touch of sand under her feet. The fog swirled away and she looked up to see Michael Barry holding her, looking down at her, the flashlight in one hand, a frown on his face.

"Damn poor time to go swimming," he said and the last bit of strength exploded inside her. "I didn't go swimming," she snapped back as the world spun away and she collapsed into his arms.

The first thing Lisa felt was warm and it was a good feeling. It told her she was alive. Slowly, her eyes closed, she allowed the process of waking to continue as her mind groped its way backwards, sorting out what had happened. The first part was reasonably clear. She had rushed down to the edge of the seawall. There was the fog and the black-robed figure on the terrace. And there had been the sound of a boat, she recalled, the sound of oars. Then there was the blow and the collision with the wall. She was pitched into the water and the rest was but a blurred series of images—the sea, floating, fighting to stay awake, and then the light and the hands pulling her to shore, Michael Barry's face frowning down at her. She opened her eyes and turned her head. Michael Barry was sitting in a leather sofa in the room, almost silhouetted against a roaring fire in a small fireplace. Her eyes traveled around the cottage. There were books against one wall and rows of cardboard boxes with excelsior stuffing piled atop one another against the other walls. It was a tight, snug little cottage, cozy and contained. She felt so warm and lazy as she stretched, the blanket smooth against her bare skin. Suddenly her eyes snapped open wider and her hand moved down her body. She was absolutely naked. She looked across the cottage at the young man on the sofa. This time she saw he was watching her, his blue eyes twinkling again with that cool, self-contained amusement, and suddenly she remembered his remark as he pulled her ashore.

"Welcome to Barry Hall," he grinned, getting to his feet. She pulled the blanket up a little further. He poured something from a bottle and handed a small glass to her.

"Drink this," he said. "It's *ouzo*, Greek brandy. Wonderful stuff but in this case strictly medicinal." She sat up, unable to keep the blanket from falling from her shoulders as she sipped the brandy. It sent probing fingers of warmth through her body.

"Your clothes are in the kitchen, drying on the stove," Michael Barry said. His grin was infuriating and she felt her nakedness beneath the blanket. "Archaeological finds are getting more interesting," he said dryly. "I hope you're not embarrassed. Taking the outer covering off things is part of our work."

"And I'm sure you enjoyed your work tonight," Lisa snapped, wishing she could be as cool as he.

"Definitely," he grinned at her. She held his eyes with a glare but finally had to relent and she felt herself breaking into a wide smile.

"You did save my life," she said sincerely. "I don't think I could have made another foot to shore."

"You might have," he said, sipping some of the *ouzo*. "But if you'd like to be eternally grateful to me that's fine. You can start by telling me what in hell you were doing out there."

Lisa took a last sip of the brandy and told the story of seeing the black-robed figure on the terrace, of going down through the house and out onto the seawall, of the blow that came from nowhere in the fog. She left out only the part about not being able to go down the terrace steps. It didn't seem important to the story. She studied his eyes as she finished, saw that they never lost their faint touch of amusement.

"You don't believe me," she said, trying not to sound petulant and not entirely succeeding.

"I believe you saw what you think you saw," he said, an infuriating note of patience in his voice. "And I know you fell into the sea."

"Fell!" Lisa almost shouted. "I was hit and knocked into the sea."

"But you didn't see anyone hit you, yet you weren't completely unconscious."

"The fog was too thick," Lisa said. "I couldn't see anything."

He was sitting on the edge of the cot on which she lay and he put his hand on her shoulder, gently. His smile lost the mocking quality for a few moments and his eyes were actually sincere. "Now hear me out, Lisa Bowen," he said. "First, you heard wailing, a kind of strange singing. It is known that the old women of the village often spend the night wailing for the dead. It's an old peasant custom here on Cyprus. The wind blows from the village and goes straight up the seawall of Orion Hall. That could well have been what you heard. As for the figure on the terrace, well, the mind has a way of seeing what it wants to see and the night and the fog can make strange shapes."

"Now I'm a victim of psychic hallucinations," she snapped, shaking his hand from her shoulder and almost dropping the blanket. "I tell you someone or something was there. I saw it. How did I land in the sea if I wasn't struck?"

She was glaring at him but it failed to make a dent in his calm, patient logic.

"Frankly, I think you fell, hit your head against a tree branch you never even saw in the fog, and thought someone had hit you," he said. "You stumbled forward, into the wall as you said, and that collision pitched you into the water."

"Is that what you think?" she said, ice coating her words. "Well, I think you can get me my clothes. I'm going back to Orion Hall. I know what I saw and what happened and I'm not going to be called a kook."

Michael got up and sighed as he looked down at her.

"You're even prettier when you're angry," he said. "And as you're terribly pretty now, you must be terribly angry."

She merely glared at him and he went out to return in moments with her clothes. He handed them to her and waited.

"Do you mind?" she shot out at him.

"No," he said. "Go right ahead."

"Dammit! Do you mind waiting outside or in the other room?" she shouted. He shrugged and grinned at her. "I mind but I'll do it," he said blandly. "I have a good memory."

She cast around for something to throw at him but there was nothing near enough and she watched him go out into the night. She flung the blanket off and flew into her clothes. It would be just like him to come back in on some pretext. But the door stayed closed until she opened it and he turned to her.

"You were going to tell me the legend of Athena," she said. He shook his head. "Why not?" she flared at once.

"I told you the villagers believed she prowls the terrace and you went and nearly got yourself killed seeing things," he said. "I'm not about to give that overactive imagination of yours anything more to feed on."

"You're an impossible, insufferable, self-satisfied ass!" she flung at him.

"Flattery will get you nowhere," he smiled at her, taking her arm. "Come on, I'll see that you get back safely."

She tried to shake loose of his grip but found that was impossible and strode off with him holding her arm, glaring up at his infuriating affableness. The fog had cleared away and the stars were bright blue-white pins stuck in a black velvet cloth. The first tint of the coming day could be seen over the edge of the horizon when they reached Orion Hall. He had followed behind her along the narrow seawall ledge and when they stepped off onto the soil he pulled her to a halt.

"This the scene of the crime?" he asked blandly at the edge of the silent, deserted terrace wall.

"It was all my imagination" she said icily and hurried on. He followed her to the big oaken door of the house and she suddenly felt a little ashamed. Perhaps she had expected too much in the way of belief.

"I'm sorry I got so angry before," she said. His eyes held their cool amusement as he looked down at her. She felt her temper flare instantly but she held it down. "All I can say is thanks for saving me."

"I've had my reward." He grinned at her and she felt her cheeks color in the dark. Her temper exploded this time.

"Dammit, you're impossible to be nice to," she snapped.

"It takes practice," he said. He was walking away before she had the door open and she went up to her room still seething. Not only had he disbelieved everything she said but he had a way of making her feel an utter fool. She crawled into the big bed and lay awake rethinking everything that had happened and she knew she hadn't imagined anything at all. She hadn't hit her head on a tree and thought someone had struck her. There *had* been someone and there had been the sound of a boat and oars. The figure on the terrace had been there. Damn Michael Barry and his calm, reasoned logic, she swore to herself. Damn him and his cool, mocking eyes. It could have been the man, Kosta, prowling about, seizing an opportunity to extract his vengeance on her. He had threatened her, had promised she would pay. Or it could have been whoever had called Maggie out onto the steamer deck to find her death in the storm-swept Mediterranean. She could no longer accept Maggie's conclusion about that. It hadn't been sleepwalking. There had been a call, cleverly arranged. She was certain now. All her first dark fears had been made real again.

Whatever had happened, whatever or whoever caused it out there in the fog this night, it had been real and she was no victim of psychic hallucination, no prey to an overactive imagination. That, she told herself firmly, was that. She also told Michael Barry to take his theories and go to hell with them. She closed her eyes tightly and absolutely refused to even think about the terrace steps.

CHAPTER FIVE

"There is no borrowing
a sword in war time."
—Cypriote Greek Proverb

In the morning Lisa woke with her mind full of unfinished, unclear wonderings. But she had decided not to say anything to Maggie about what had happened during the night. The chances were that Maggie, with her factual approach to life, wouldn't believe her any more than Michael Barry had. Until she had something unrefutable, something concrete, she would stay quiet. Except for Demetrius, she mused while dressing. She might speak to him of what had happened. He would at least listen with an open mind, she felt certain, and she looked forward to seeing his Grecian handsomeness again. She felt the need for someone to understand. And Demetrius was both understanding and exciting and that was something to look forward to, also. He certainly would be a welcome relief after her last session with Michael Barry, she told herself, and twinkling, mocking blue eyes flashed through her mind. Now she understood Michael's words about believing everything and nothing. He was a complete and total cynic and she was annoyed at herself for even thinking about him, but he had lodged himself like an irritating cinder in the mind's eye.

She dressed in a minikilt and a sleeveless blouse of pale yellow. The sun streaming through the window was already hot and she hurried downstairs to help Maggie until Demetrius arrived. Maggie and Thera were just outside the big main door and Lisa joined them as the old man, Nikos, drove up in a two-wheeled cart pulled by a donkey.

"It's his," Maggie explained. "I told him to bring it up here and put it in the stables around the back. I didn't know there were stables until Nikos mentioned them to me. You know, we've concentrated on the center of the house but there's a lot to this place we haven't even investigated yet. The rooms in the turrets, for instance."

Maggie was right, of course. The two rooms they had taken over seemed like former guest rooms more than anything else and suddenly Lisa realized that the last Mistress of Orion Hall must have had a master room of her own, something grand and impressive, and it was somewhere here in this vast house. Maggie cut into her thoughts.

"Tell Nikos I want him to use his cart to gather firewood all morning," she said. "Tell him I want lots and lots of it stacked up in the bam. You know, my dear, we'll need it. Everything in this old place is heated by fire. Even the kitchen stoves are woodbuming."

There was a grim annoyance in the older woman's voice and Lisa put her hand on Maggie's arm. "Sorry you decided on this whole thing, on coming here?" she asked gently.

"No," Maggie said quickly. "Once I get settled I'll be fine. A little primitiveness is good for one. I've always felt we live with too many luxuries nowadays, anyway."

Rationalization? Lisa wondered. She smiled inwardly. It didn't really matter so long as it helped. She gave Nikos Maggie's instructions and watched the old man wheel the little donkey cart around and start down the road. Then she went inside and helped Maggie unwrap three large bundles of old drapes that, they both decided, were too faded and aged for use. It was a little past eleven o'clock when Demetrius arrived, looking even more as though he had just stepped from the games at ancient Athens, a fugitive from history's pages. His dark handsomeness was made more so by a white, loose-fitting blouse that hung open down the front, crisscrossed only by thin, leather thongs. He carried a large wicker picnic basket covered over with white tissue paper and Lisa saw his deep eyes take in her own long, supple body. He whisked the tissue paper from the basket and handed Lisa a bright yellow sunbonnet, its brim trimmed with little red and blue flowers made of straw.

"For you, to wear on our picnic," he said. "And whenever you go out in the Cyprus sun."

Lisa felt a rush of warmth and she was touched. She would have reached up to kiss him but Maggie appeared and she held back, knowing he would see the promise in her eyes. Demetrius shot Maggie a particularly dazzling smile as he gave her a short bow.

"The sun here on Cyprus is deceptive," he explained. "It seems gentle but it can bake you like a potato. The next time I come I will bring you one."

"I've got one I used to wear gardening back in Sussex," Maggie said. "I've got to dig it out of my trunk. But thank you for the thought." Maggie's eyes, Lisa saw, studied Demetrius with a sharp gaze though her smile stayed warm. Her aunt really didn't trust handsome men, Lisa noted, and smiled inwardly. A really handsome man had no doubt hurt her many years ago. She turned to see Thera in the corridor, her eyes bright with admiration as she gazed at the sunbonnet.

"It is beautiful," she whispered to Lisa. "The most beautiful bonnet I have ever seen. So bright and gay."

"I bought it in Famagusta when I was there yesterday," Demetrius said. "I shall get another bright one the next time I go. There was only one like that."

"And I love it," Lisa said, adjusting it on her head. "Are we ready for our picnic?"

"Most ready," Demetrius said, his warm smile lighting the dark corridor and foyer. His hand found hers and Lisa left with him, taking a moment to shoot Maggie a wink. Maggie's eyes were thoughtful, watching them go. Demetrius led her halfway through the town and then cut off onto a small road that rose gently and afforded a beautiful view of the stone quay at the waterfront where the *panigyri* had been held. As they walked on and the road climbed higher Demetrius paused to point his arm eastward across the Mediterranean. "Syria lies that way," he said, "not very far away. And Turkey to the north." He stood for a moment, his eyes narrowed, gazing east toward Syria, almost as though he could see the land. But there was only the blue and, from there, flat expanse of the Mediterranean and his hand closed over Lisa's again. He led her up a narrow trail, leaving the road suddenly, and at a small rise she saw the white towers of a Gothic structure on a distant hilltop.

"Built by the Crusaders," Demetrius said. "Still run by the Carpathian friars. There are mosques here, too, built by Haroun-al-Raschid, and Hellenic temples erected by Alexander."

"And you, as a modem Greek man, what do you think of all these different cultures that have marked Cyprus forever?"

His eyes seemed to harden for a brief instant but she might have imagined it, she knew, for his dazzling smile was equally instantaneous. "As a Greek I follow in the footsteps of my ancestors." He smiled. "I believe, like Socrates who said he was not an

Athenian or a Greek but a citizen of the world, that it is best to accommodate to all life's fortunes and turns."

He turned and led her to still another hill and sat down almost at the very top of it, putting the basket next to him. She lowered herself beside him and in brilliant sunlight they looked down on the whole long finger of the island that pointed eastward to unseen Syria. It was an eagle's view and breathtaking. She was glad for the sunbonnet as the sun beat down harshly and only the soft wind offered cooling relief. Demetrius opened the wicker basket and she saw he had brought chicken legs, sausage and salami, olives and grapes, and thick Greek wheat bread. He brought forth a chilled bottle of Mavrodaphne, a sweet red wine perfect for the highly spiced sausages and seasoned chicken. He also produced a small, leather-covered flask of Metaxa brandy and they ate and drank and talked under the warm, enervating sun. The wine and the brandy making the world a deliciously soft, carefree place, Lisa lay back in the grass and looked up at Demetrius, at the handsome chiseled profile, the sensuous lips. He was watching a hawk slowly wheel in the sky.

"I love to watch the hawk," he said. "They do not fly about aimlessly. They wait until an opportunity comes and then they take it, ruthlessly, instantly. They let nothing interfere with the business at hand, which is, for them, to kill."

"That sounds so cold and deadly," Lisa said. "I guess you used the right word, ruthless. It doesn't sound like the kind of thing you'd admire."

"Every man has some cruelty in him, I suppose," he said, turning and looking down at her, his strong face just above hers. The virile, animal sensuousness of the man seized her in a silent grip and his lips moved down to cover hers, pressing hard against her mouth. Her lips opened and her arms encircled his neck, smooth and thick as a Doric column. His hand was moving against the skin of her neck and she felt the buttons of her blouse come open, his touch exciting, electric. Her body strained upwards toward his, her flesh wanting with a will of its own.

"You are so beautiful," he murmured through his caresses. "Too beautiful." Dimly she wondered at the sadness of his words and then his lips were moving against hers again, harder this time, almost frightening, as though he had suddenly changed into another person. But his touch moved her body forward once more and then she heard the noise, the sound of loose stones being knocked against and rattling down the hillside. She pulled free and sat up, buttoning the opened buttons of her blouse.

"Someone's coming," she said. "Over on the other side of the hill." Demetrius nodded and she saw the momentary line of annoyance as his lips set together tightly, surprisingly harsh. He poured himself some brandy as Lisa looked back at the top of the hill where the sounds of someone approaching grew louder. As she watched a head appeared, reddish hair hardly combed followed by bright blue eyes that peeked over the rise. Now she felt her own jaw tighten in surprised annoyance.

"Well, this is a bit of a surprise, isn't it?" Michael Barry said coming over the rise, his wide grin creasing his face. Lisa knew she was glaring at him and she didn't care. She saw his eyes sweep the picnic basket, the wine and brandy flask and Demetrius, all in one fast glance.

"Wonderful spot for a picnic," he said, moving down to where they sat, his face the mirror of affable pleasantness.

"Demetrius, this is Michael Barry," Lisa said stiffly.

"Ah, yes, the archaeologist who lives in the cottage," Demetrius said. His smile for Michael was so warm Lisa wondered how he could be so well-mannered. She couldn't think of anyone she would have less wanted to see than Michael Barry.

"What a bright, charming bonnet," Michael said, kneeling down beside her.

"Demetrius gave it to me this morning," she said smugly and wondered fleetingly why she took such pleasure in telling that to Michael Barry. Michael's blue eyes held hers with that infuriating, mocking amusement in them that seemed to say he knew they'd been making love on the hillside and that he knew just what was going on inside her.

"How is your archaeological work coming here on Cyprus?" Demetrius asked Michael. "Getting anything really good?"

"Quite a bit," Michael said blandly. "Found a most unusual item last night. I haven't really classified it yet. Beautiful little figure."

Lisa managed to keep her face expressionless but her eyes, fastened on Michael, were pinpoints of fury. He shot her a bland smile, ignoring her eyes.

"I should like to see the little figure you found sometime," Demetrius said innocently. Michael gave him a broad grin that included Lisa.

"You very likely will," he said. Lisa wanted to slap him so hard that her hand trembled.

"Some wine?" Demetrius offered politely.

"No, thanks," Michael said, getting to his feet. "It makes me see things."

You bastard, Lisa said silently. He tossed Lisa another smile, affable on the surface, filled with mocking laughter inside.

"It was fun meeting you," he said briskly. "But I must get on. I've some digging to do yet today."

He went off with a final, cheery wave of his hand and Lisa watched his figure till it disappeared onto one of the small roads further down the hillside. She was seething inside though she tried to appear calm as she lay back and put her hand on Demetrius. He turned and studied her, stroking her hair with one hand. She tried putting her arms around him but then she drew back. It was no use. Their entire moment had been shattered, the lovely mood exploded. All by that archaeological oaf, she swore inwardly. She was angry at him and at herself for feeling this way and she sat up sullenly.

"Seeing that fellow has upset you," Demetrius said, half question and half comment. "Does he mean anything to you?"

"Good God, no!" Lisa said quickly, as though the mere thought was blasphemous. She threw out the first explanation that popped into her mind. "Cynical people always upset me," she said. "And he made me think of last night and I've been trying not to think of last night."

She had still been wavering about whether to tell Demetrius but now she wanted very much to tell him and suddenly she realized that he might know the legend of Athena. Holding fast to his strong hand she told him what had happened during the night, of the shadowed figure on the terrace, of the unseen blow, of how she'd floated beyond the point and had managed to get ashore. She said Michael Barry had helped her get back but she skipped the part about waking up in his cottage without a stitch on under the blanket. That really wasn't at all important to the story anyway, she decided. When she finished Demetrius gazed at her with concern, his hands closed around hers.

"What a terrible experience, Lisa my darling," he said. The deep liquid depths of his eyes were troubled and it was obvious that he, for one, didn't treat her story as that of psychic hallucinations.

"It was someone, Demetrius," she said, "someone who tried to kill me. Do you think it could have been that man Kosta?

I told you about standing up to him over Thera. He threatened me then."

Demetrius' classic profile turned and stared away for a moment. "I doubt it was Kosta," he said. "The man has anger but it comes from fear and shame. I do not think he could kill."

Lisa saw those burning, piercing eyes in her mind and was far from sure he could not and would not kill. But she didn't argue the point. Instead she pressed Demetrius further.

"I have been told the villagers believe that the spirit of Athena, the last Mistress of Orion Hall, still prowls the lower terrace on fogbound nights waiting for vengeance of some kind," she said. "What is the legend of Athena, Demetrius? I saw her portrait in the cellar and I know now why so many of the people stared at me. I look almost exactly like her. But I saw fear in their eyes. It must have something to do with the legend. Can you tell me about it?"

He pursed his lips and looked at her with narrowed eyes.

"Yes, I can tell you the legend of Athena," he said. "And it is true that many of the people of the village still believe she prowls on the nights of the fog. The older ones believe it as a certain truth. Many of the younger ones listened and wondered. It is forbidden to scoff at the beliefs of your elders here on Cyprus. But of late the sound of her strange wailing cries have been heard more and more. There are few, now, in all the village who would dare to scoff at the legend."

"And why do they fear the legend?" Lisa asked. "I want to know the whole story."

Demetrius sat back, reluctance tinging his face, but he spoke to her in flat, emotionless tones. "Athena was a girl here in Caramania of indescribable beauty," he began. "But she had a terrible temper and those who crossed her soon had unexplainable accidents. Belief in the existence of witches was common everywhere in those days. But they were not sure she was a witch so they banished her from the island. While she was on Rhodes, she met and married a rich young Englishman."

Lisa nodded. That, of course, would be Richard Willis, her great-grandfather.

"Athena returned to Cyprus and to Caramania as his bride," Demetrius went on. "He built Orion Hall for her. Not long after it was finished he was killed in an accident and Athena became the Mistress and ruler of Orion Hall. The legend has it that she began to reveal herself as a true witch and exercised terrible power over the people of the village. That portrait you saw used to hang in the town meetinghouse, put there by Athena to remind the people of her presence. Finally, according to the legend, things grew so bad that the people gathered the courage to kill her. It was known that on fogbound nights she prowled the dark and so one night a handful of the bravest men went out to slay her. It was necessary, according to the traditions of such things, that they kill her with their own hands. Only then, when they took her life themselves, would the spirit of evil inside her die along with her. But she fled from them in the fog, laughing at them, and somehow or other she fell from the east turret, from the very top, and was killed. But she had cheated them nevertheless. Athena was dead but because they had not slain her with their own hands, the spirit of evil within her, her spirit, still lived. The legend has it that they went back to their homes knowing that they would be cursed forever. And ever since, according to the legend, the spirit of Athena has prowled the terrace on the fogbound nights, for it was such a night her body was killed. She calls and wails, daring someone to come to face her vengeance. And of course, at such times, the people fasten their shutters and lock their doors tightly."

Demetrius fell silent and Lisa felt a chill course through her body despite the hot glare of the sun.

"But it's only a legend, of course," she said, watching the man's classic face. "The part about her being a witch, I mean, and evil spirits that prowl in the night."

The man said nothing and Lisa frowned. "Surely you don't believe such things," she said.

Demetrius shrugged. "No, I cannot in all honesty say I believe in such things," he admitted. "And yet you yourself say you do not know what you saw last night. You saw something, and yet there was nothing. I only know it makes one stop and wonder."

Lisa shook her head impatiently. The whole thing was ridiculous, of course. Only, and her jaw tightened, she really had no explanation for last night. There had been something, and yet nothing, something there but not there. A blow felt but from out of the night and the fog, from an unseen hand. She shook herself and knew she had to get away, alone, to think this strange and chilling business out on her own.

"Take me back, Demetrius," she said quietly, putting the sunbonnet forward on her head. He turned and cupped her face in his hands.

"As you wish, but first, Lisa, let me say this to you," he said, his eyes holding hers. "I do not pretend to understand all these things. This is a strange world we live in. But I do know that I have come to care much for you in a short time and perhaps you are in danger. Perhaps it was the man Kosta. I cannot even be sure of that. But I think you and your aunt should leave here, for your safety. That is my first concern."

"Maggie won't go," Lisa said. She was absolutely certain of that without really knowing why.

"Why not? Why won't she?" Demetrius said, his question so sharp that it startled her.

"I don't know," she answered honestly. "I just know she won't go."

"Then you will go, my sweet one," he said. "I will arrange my affairs so we can meet in Athens or Venice or London, wherever you wish. I want very much to see you away from here."

His hands on her arms pressed tightly, comfortingly. "I'll have to think about it, Demetrius," she said.

"I speak for your good, Lisa," he said. "No, I will change that. I speak for our good. Perhaps what happened was just something that will never be explained. And then perhaps there is danger for you here. The important thing is not to risk your life, my darling."

He folded her arm in his and she clung to him as they started down the hillside. At least here was deep concern and not cynicism and she was moved and grateful for it. When they reached the doorway of Orion Hall, Thera was outside clipping off overgrown vines. Lisa saw the girl's eyes caress the sunbonnet again enviously. She kissed Demetrius quickly on the cheek and hurried inside and to her room. Whipping off the sunbonnet she threw herself on the bed and stared up at the ceiling. Her mind swam with dark thoughts and she fought to sort them out, to make sense out of what made no sense. And, as she tried to arrange what she had experienced and had heard in some kind of cohesive order, she began to realize that she herself was being torn by a strange, inner straggle. She wanted facts, yet she felt herself drawn to the dark mysteries of the unknown. Witches, spells, evil spirits, these things were ridiculous, ancient superstitions. They were, indeed, legends. They weren't real. Even when people believed in these things they weren't real, she told herself. But then, the question sprang up at her, what makes a thing real if not believing in it? Where did legends end and reality begin? Was there a clean dividing line? Greek history and story and drama was filled with these unreal beliefs. Sophocles, Euripedes, Aeschylus, and all the other great Greek dramatists, cornerstones of all drama that has come since, used witches and curses and the spirit of evil as an accepted fact of life. But, of course, it was so accepted in those ancient days. Much that was unreal was believed as completely real, things we laugh at today. Yet, she wondered, do we laugh only because we dare not look too closely? She recalled Maggie's words about the Greek in her, her imagination drawn to the dark and unknown, and she got up, angry at herself, and paced the room.

It was ridiculous, the whole idiotic business, she told herself. Her other self angrily pulled at her. She was a modern girl from Vermont, educated to think clearly. Thought, reason, light, not dark imaginings, were what was needed. She sorted out events once again in her mind as she paced the room. She had seen something, that much she clung to. But she had to admit it could have been any robed figure. She could even have imagined it was robed in black when in reality it was just someone else there, such as Kosta. She thought back again to the very beginning of it all. It was he who had stood outside the hotel in London. She was convinced of that now. And then there was the little lawyer, and once again she saw the cold, deadly glitter of the man's eyes. And the accident with the crane on the dock at Piraeus. Was that really an accident? And then, of course, that business with Maggie aboard the ship. That was no longer a question mark in her mind. Her suspicions had become certainties. Certainties! The word struck at her like a blow and she sat down on the bed, suddenly very depressed. There were no certainties, dammit, she had to admit. Or very few. Everything that had happened was clouded in uncertainty. Everything *could* have been accidental. Maggie could have been sleepwalking. Kosta could have been outside the hotel watching her and Maggie or it could have been someone else. Or he could have been there but on business of his own. He might have been waiting there for someone else. She could have seen a figure on the terrace, and she felt sure she had, but Michael Barry could have been right. Her imagination could have run off with her, much as the thought made her furious. And so, in cold examination, there were no certainties. The only hard facts she had were so strange that they didn't fit anywhere—her fear of the terrace steps and of the pomegranates the old woman had pushed at her. They were facts, those fears, but unexplainable, incomprehensible, unreal of themselves.

Lisa got up and hurried down the wide stairway and out of the house. Maybe a good walk would help relieve the tension inside her, she told herself. It was this island that added to her inner confusion, to the whole eerie affair. The people on it lived in awe of the unknown, afraid of forces greater than they, born and bred with a heritage of dark terrors. It was a place carved out of contrasts, fed by the legends of many cultures, and wrapped in superstitions. It resisted logic and tried to bury reason under a blanket of ancient beliefs in a climate of fear. But these super-stitions, these legends, were not abstractions. They touched her, somehow. Foolish as they might be, they reached out to touch her as if they were real and, in a way, that made them real. Lisa had walked quickly, head down, and now she found herself along the stone quay of the town's seafront. She paused to look at the three fishing dories tied to the quay and thought of the sound of a rowboat she had heard during the night. Still in her cloud of thoughts, she heard the voice from nearby.

"This must be my lucky day," it said and she turned to see Michael Barry sitting at a small marble table outside a coffee-house. His grin, full of insouciance, triggered her memory of the hillside and her temper, both at once. She stalked over to him and he pulled a chair out for her.

THE MISTRESS OF ORION HALL

"Join me in a cup of good, strong Turkish coffee," he said blandly. "This is the only place around here that serves it." He gestured to a man who poked his head out of the door. "Another cup of *qahwah*, please," he said.

"I'm not joining you in anything," Lisa snapped, her brown eyes darkened with anger. "I suppose you thought that exhibition you put on before was funny."

He frowned in mock protest, his blue eyes twinkling. "What exhibition?" he said. "I enjoyed bumping into you and your friend Demetrius."

"All those smart-ass remarks about your archaeological discovery last night," Lisa huffed.

"Oh, that." He smiled. "Come now, where's your sense of humor, my girl?"

"I'm not your girl and I wouldn't be for anything," Lisa flung at him. "And I'm afraid my sense of humor isn't improved by being laughed at and treated like some silly child."

He pursed his lips and gave her a long sideways glance, and his blue eyes lost their mocking laughter for a moment. They were almost understanding, she saw in surprise.

"You're still sure someone was on the terrace last night?" he asked quietly. "You're still convinced someone hit you from behind?"

Lisa's lips tightened and a sudden rush of despair flooded over her. Angry at the tears that welled up into her eyes, she cast out her words in bitterness.

"I don't know what I'm sure of anymore," she said, turning her head away and waiting to hear some cynical remark, gloating or mocking. But Michael said nothing and she was grateful for that. And surprised. He did have some vestigial sensitivity, perhaps. The man brought the *qahwah* and she took a large sip of it. Hot, it was both bitter and sweet and terribly strong and she felt her eyes blinking. Michael, sipping his slowly, watched her with a small smile edging his lips.

"What caused this sudden lack of certainty?" he finally asked and she shrugged helplessly.

"I'm certain one moment and then not the next," she said. "I think maybe it's this place. But I know the legend of Athena now." She couldn't keep the note of smug triumph out of her voice and she was annoyed that he seemed only curious and not chastened.

"Oh?" Michael said, a rising note of questioning appraisal in the one word. "Your friend Demetrius tell it to you?"

She nodded and proceeded to tell him everything Demetrius had told her, watching his face intently as she did. But he kept a bland, irritatingly frustrating, expressionless mask on. When she finished Michael nodded and his eyes studied her speculatively.

"He left out a few details," he said slowly. "Maybe he figured they were unimportant. Or maybe he doesn't know them."

"What kind of details?" Lisa asked, her curiosity aroused at once. "He told me that Athena fell to her death from the east turret. I'd say that was quite detailed."

"No," Michael said flatly. "He left out the kind of details that lets you sort out the facts from the embroidery, that lets you separate history from legend. You see, in archaeology that's one of the first things we learn to do because most all legends contain some fact. The kind of facts, how many of them, and what they mean tell you about the nature of reality."

"What did he leave out?" Lisa pressed. "Seeing that I know the legend now, or most of it, you don't have to worry about stimulating my overactive imagination." She let the icy sarcasm hang on her words and saw the amused light of response in Michael Barry's eyes.

"For one thing, Athena's husband, Richard Willis, wasn't killed in an accident," Michael said, toying with his coffee.

"Evidence put together later showed that he was murdered by Athena."

Lisa's eyebrows shot upward.

"That's right," Michael said. "When his body was recovered, a local doctor made a stomach analysis and found that Richard Willis had been poisoned. Of course, the doctor was in fear for his own life and left secret notes only discovered fifty years later. It seems that Athena had fed her husband pomegranates poisoned with strychnine. Then she dragged his body down the steps at the rear of the terraces until she reached the bottom terrace. She threw the body over the seawall from there. The tide was supposed to wash it out to sea but it caught on a submerged rock and was discovered and brought ashore the next day."

Michael stopped and frowned at Lisa. She was sitting frozen, her face ashen. Inside her body there was only numbing coldness as his words burned in her mind. She felt herself get to her feet, almost as if in a dream. The little table was spinning. Michael Barry was wavering, appearing and disappearing before her eyes. All she could feel and see and hear were his words of the pomegranates and the terrace steps.

"I've got to go," she said, hearing her own voice strained, tight. "I've got to be alone."

She turned and started to run, back to Orion Hall, fleeing like a frightened deer, and she heard Michael call after her but she kept running, along the quay, up through a narrow street, on toward the big house at the end of the village. She reached the oaken door, glanced back to see Michael running after her, and slammed the door shut behind her. She dashed up the stairs, seeing nothing, running as though she were on a cloud, and fell onto the bed in her room. She was shaking and cold and her fingers clutched the bedspread, pulling it into small knots. Things like this don't happen, she said to herself. They don't, they don't, she repeated, hearing her voice saying it over and over in a hoarse whisper. She felt the wetness of tears staining her cheeks and she turned on her back to stare up at the ceiling. No amount of frantic denial would help, she knew, for it had happened, the unreasoning, numbing, sickening fear of the pomegranates and of the terrace steps. She had known without knowing. From out of the dark and terrible past something had reached out to her and now she knew, once and for all, that whatever was happening here at Orion Hall, she was more than a bystander. The knowledge curdled her blood and seized her in a withering grasp. The past had no claims on the present. The past could not reach out to make old legends come alive. Everyone knew that, except that it had happened, and she cringed with a terrible fear, the fear that comes with realizing that there are forces beyond man's knowledge, that the unknown can be as real as the known. There were no irrational fears, no ominous imaginings she could conjure up that could match what had happened. Not so long ago, before modern man became so cynical, and certainly in the days of the ancient Greek civilization, good and evil were not mere words. Evil was a real thing, a tangible entity, a spirit that had a life and a force of its own. It wasn't merely a name for things people did. Evil was something that *was* and now, as she lay there, she knew she was no longer sure of the nature of evil. Perhaps the ancient wisdom was wiser than we know and there exists a dark force called evil. Did terrible deeds leave their claims on the souls of those that followed? The questions tumbled through her mind, one after another, each one more tortured than the other, and none held an answer. The only thing she knew was that the fear of the pomegranates and of the terrace steps had been there, inside her, as real as real can be and its roots were in the midnight of her soul and the unfathomable shadows of the past.

She heard Maggie's voice calling her and she got up from the bed. "There's a gentleman here to see you, Lisa," Maggie was calling and Lisa went downstairs, knowing it would be Michael. She'd dried her eyes and now there was a terrible resignation inside her. Michael stood just inside the thick front door, his blue eyes clouded, watching Lisa as she approached.

"I started back to my place," he said. "I told myself it was just your crazy temper but I knew better and I had to come back. I kept seeing the way your face drained itself of color. Was it because I told you Athena murdered her husband?"

Lisa looked at him steadily and then finally replied, her voice flat, her tone dead.

"No, that wasn't it," she said. "Not really. It was pomegranates and terrace steps." She saw his frown deepen and she told him what had happened to her, of the old crone and the fruit and of the successive times she tried to go down the steps. She told him with that terrible acceptance inside her and when she was finished she saw his eyes studying hers, probing their dark brown.

"Explain that to me," she said bitterly. "How does that fit under psychic hallucinations? How can even an overactive imagination work on something it never knew about? You who reconstruct reality from legend, who separate history from embroidery, tell me what that means."

Michael's eyes held no mocking humor now and his shoulders lifted helplessly. "I can't," he said. "I promised you information. You're asking for wisdom."

"I guess so," Lisa said quietly and turned to go back up the wide stairs. "Good night, Michael," she said.

"Lisa," he called and she paused at the bottom step, not turning. "I'll work on it," he said. "Let's not go off the deep end just because there's something you can't explain. Hear me?"

"I hear you," she said. "Good night, Michael." She was almost to the top of the stairs before she heard the door open and Michael leave. It was strange how suddenly so many of the little things fell into place now, and she recalled how she had seemed to know Orion Hall the moment she saw it, how the huge, forbidding, frightening old house had drawn her to it in a strange way. And she knew something else. Whatever was here, whatever the dark forces were that reached out to her, would have to be met by her and her alone. Demetrius' concern and care, Michael Barry's tempered cynicism, Maggie's adherence to hard facts, none of these could help her. Nothing had been made clear. Uncertainties, mystery, the unexplained and the unknown had, if anything, been deepened. But she had been touched as she had not been touched before. And that was her burden now. Whatever else might be, that was hers to carry, to unravel or to never know.

Lisa succeeded in being at least a shell of her usual self at dinner and as Maggie had reached the end of her day's energies, the evening ended early. Lisa went to her room and lay down on the bed. The thoughts in her mind had stopped whirling and an almost calm determination had replaced them. She knew the first thing she had to do. If the past reached out to touch her, perhaps the answers could be found if she tried to touch the past. If she could, it might carry its own message. And if she could not, perhaps the dark shadows that had come to cloak her heart had a lining of hope. Perhaps. She lay quietly and listened to the night grow older. When the house was silent and she was certain everyone else slept she rose and went outside and down the staircase. She took one of the kerosene lamps from the dining hall. The light cast tall shapes on the stone walls as she moved toward the east turret. It was from there Athena had fallen to her death, Demetrius had told her. Had she gone to hide in her room? Or had she gone there to get a weapon, to take up a position from where she could fight off her attackers? Whatever it had been, it was one place where she could perhaps touch the past, Lisa knew, and her footsteps were drawn to the great convex walls of the east turret as surely as though a magnet pulled them.

The lamp cast its yellow circle of light ahead of her as she ascended the few steps to the rounded walls of the turret and to the wooden door there. The heavy bolt of iron barely moved as she pushed against it. Setting down the lamp she seized the handle with both hands and pushed with all her strength. It gave way reluctantly, as though it were unwilling to offer up its secrets, but finally the door stood open and she pulled it wide. Lamp in hand, she entered the turret and looked at the circular steps winding their way upward, dark and dusty. Here was one place no one had entered since it had been shut. A strange excitement seizing her, she began to climb the steps. They went up in a slow circle following the wall and suddenly she came to a landing and a closed doorway. The steps continued on above it but Lisa stopped and approached the door, her heart pounding. Here, unlike the rest of the house, there were cobwebs and spiders and the air of places long closed. She pushed against the door and it opened stiffly. She pushed again, exerting a steady pressure, and the door opened all the way, scraping against the stone of the floor, sending small mounds of dust rolling aside.

Lisa held the lamp high in front of her and saw that she stood at the threshold of a huge, circular room with convex windows at the far end. A dressing table stood to one side and there was a three-candle holder on it. The girl moved to the table and picked up the holder, lighting the candles with the flame of the lamp. They sent shafts of light into the room at once as she set them back onto the table. She saw another lamp on a dark dresser but knew that any kerosene in it would be dried up by now. There were more candles at the end of the dresser and she lit them quickly. The huge room took shape now and she gazed at the wide bed with a high headboard that stood at the far side of the room. The candles sent out their flickering light and with the glow of her lamp, the room was lighted well enough to see. Two low tables topped with slabs of marble stood facing each other across the center of the round floor. Dust-covered books lined a shelf against part of the wall and a walk-in closet stood open nearby. Lisa went over to it and touched the dresses that hung there—long robes, some of velvet, most of silk and wool. A dress caught her eye, white and flowing, and she pulled it from the closet. It was the dress of the portrait in the cellar. She held it against her and saw that it would be a perfect fit. Putting it back in the closet she walked to the dressing table. There were jars of ointments still waiting to be used, a glistening brooch of emeralds, and a necklace of hammered gold leaves, Egyptian in flavor. A hairbrush, glazed ceramic back and handle, lay beside a small jewelry box. She opened the box and her eyes traveled over the collection of rings and pendants and earrings. Her hand reached out and took a ring, a huge stone of jade set in a coiled serpent of silver. The ring slipped on her finger as though it had been fashioned for her and she turned around to gaze at the room, her form outlined by the candlelight against the smooth stone walls that curved around her almost protectively. Athena, the Mistress of Orion Hall, was still here in this vast room. Her presence was in the air, ominous yet enticing, repelling yet commanding, and from some tiny spot in Lisa's mind she heard the lines from Shelley's "Adonais" and she spoke them softly in the dim light.

Winged persuasions and veiled Destinies,
  Splendors and Glooms and glimmering Incarnations
Of hopes and fears and twilight fantasies.

There were winged persuasions here in this room. She could feel them vibrating inside her and she shrank from the thought of what veiled destinies they offered.

She rubbed the smooth coldness of the ring with her fingers and then took the lamp into her hand. Its light made the coiled serpent of silver shine and the jade flash green fire. She walked from the room and ascended the rest of the circular stairs, walking slowly, deliberately. Not too far on she came to the closed door at the top of the turret. It opened easily as she pressed against it and she was standing outside, on the parapet of the turret. The wind clutched at her at once with invisible hands and she lifted her face to look at the star-swept sky. Here was where Athena had come, up the winding steps, to mock her attackers from the top of the turret. The stone parapet that circled the turret was low, Lisa saw, coming up only a little higher than her knees. And yet Athena must have known this and been aware of the danger of it. Lisa walked from the doorway, moving slowly around the narrow balcony that circled the turret. The wind was chilling and she felt herself growing cold and suddenly she feared the lamp would blow out. Quickening her pace she hurried on to complete her circle of the turret. She was just returning to the front, high above the Mediterranean, when she was flung forward as though a giant hand had pushed her. She screamed and heard her scream taken by the wind and carried off into the night and then her legs hit the low top of the parapet and she was falling forward, over the edge, hurtling to her death. Desperately she flung out her arms and felt the stone top of the parapet. She closed her arm around it and felt her body swing hard, hitting the edge of it, and she didn't dare look down. The pull of the wind told her she hung from the side with only the grip of her arm pressed against the top of the parapet between her and death. She pressed her arm tighter and brought her other hand around, slowly, careful not to dislodge her precarious hold by a sudden shift of balance. Her hand slid on the smooth stone but she reached out enough to curl her fingers around the far edge and pull. Her arm was growing numb quickly and she knew it would soon lose its strength. She pulled upwards and managed to lift herself over the parapet enough to lean on top of it and draw in deep drafts of air. Then, pressing down with her hands, she pushed herself up a few inches more and got a leg halfway over the edge of the stones. Once again she rested and caught her breath. Still being careful not to make sudden moves, she pulled herself up again until she got one leg entirely upon the parapet edge and then and only then did she move quickly, throwing herself down to the balcony of the turret to lay there, her heart pounding furiously in her breast.

The shattered glass of the kerosene lamp lay just ahead, a grim marker of how death's hands had clutched at her. Lisa sat up and then pulled herself to her feet. Now, for the first time, she could wonder at what had happened, for once again an unseen force had struck at her. Turning in the direction she had come she peered at the balcony curving emptily about the roundness of the turret. Cautiously she started back, retracing her path. She put one foot out at a time, testing each step, and then, suddenly, her foot turned under her and she felt the loose stone dip as she pressed down on it. She pressed again and one end of it went down like a child's see-saw. That was what had done it. Coming from the other direction she had stepped on it and had been pitched forward, the low edge of the parapet catching her just above the knees to send her hurtling over the edge. She closed her eyes and saw the black-robed figure of Athena hurtling over the parapet, her screams rending the night, just as her own had. Kneeling down she examined the stone. It had simply come loose and it moved as on a hinge when pressure was put upon it. Only the stiffness of years of accumulated dirt had stopped it from turning more quickly. If it had, the added impetus would surely have sent her flying from the turret too forcefully to grasp the ledge. She got up, carefully avoiding the stone, and retrieved the darkened lamp. At the door leading from the turret she looked back and shuddered. She had uncovered a fact, the fact of how Athena, Mistress of Orion Hall, had fallen to her death, one of those facts that Michael Barry said lay inside every legend. But it was also a fact that twice she had narrowly escaped death and both times the spirit of Athena had been there. Each time something had made her go in search and each time death had lain in wait. A coincidence? Or "winged persuasions and veiled destinies?" Lisa almost smiled to herself. Whatever the reasons, until she found out she knew she would live with the legend of Athena as a part of her very inner being.

She closed the door and went down the steps, led by the glow of the candlelight from the big circular room not far below. When she reached it she stopped and blew out the candles and wished she could blow out the cold fear inside her as easily. Closing the door she made her way down the circular stone stairs in complete and total blackness, holding the broken lamp in one hand, the only sound the beating of her heart. Finally she reached the bottom and emerged from the turret into the house, bolting the door after her. She went to her room and fell onto the bed and sleep came over her almost at once, the sweet refuge of the troubled mind and the tortured soul.

CHAPTER SIX

"Every gypsy praises his own basket."
—Cypriote Greek Proverb

L ISA WOKE, surprised at how refreshed she felt. She had slept
soundly for a change. As she lay in bed she felt the smooth
stone on her finger and sat up on one elbow to look at the ring. It
was beautiful but she wished it hadn't fit so perfectly on her hand,
as though it were a sign of her bond to the beautiful girl in the
portrait. She took it off and put it in the drawer of the dresser and
hurried into her clothes, pausing only to wash quickly. The warm
brilliance of the morning sun made dark legends and witches
and somber thoughts of evil seem completely ridiculous and
terribly remote. Perhaps that was why she decided to say nothing
to Maggie of what had happened during the night. Besides, she
still had too many threads to unravel before speaking of her fears
and wonderings. She explained the shattered glass by saying
she had gone downstairs to investigate a noise and had dropped
the lamp.

Maggie had tasks planned for everyone as soon as breakfast
was done with, but before Lisa sat down to coffee Demetrius
arrived looking positively formal in jacket and trousers and
black shoes. He spoke to Lisa at the doorway, his hand closing
on hers.

"I must go to Kyrenia this morning," he said. "But I will be back this afternoon. I just wanted to see you before I left and to tell you to think about what I asked you to do."

"I have," Lisa said. "And I can't leave now. There are too many things here I must do yet and too many things I must learn."

His hand tightened on hers and she saw his jaw grow taut for a brief moment. "We will talk some more of this," he said. Then his handsome face broke into a warm caress of a smile. "If you go out today, do not forget your sunbonnet," he said. "The sun is already burning."

"I wouldn't think of it," Lisa laughed and stood very still as he bent down and brushed her ear with his lips. Then he was gone, hurrying away, and she went back to the breakfast table in the big kitchen. Maggie was talking to Thera and hastened to have Lisa explain things to Nikos, who stood by. Maggie wanted to know where bathroom fixtures might be purchased to replace most of those in the house that were rusted. Nikos thought that Yialousa might be the nearest place. But because Maggie wanted the old man to stay at Orion Hall and help with the furniture polishing, it was finally arranged that Thera would use his cart and mule for the trip.

"But first she's going to give your room a fast cleaning," Maggie said to Lisa. "The trip to Yialousa will take long enough and I'd rather get the cleaning out of the way before."

"I'll give her a hand with my room. It'll be quicker that way," Lisa said and Maggie nodded her appreciation. Breakfast over, Lisa hurried to her room, picked up loose clothes, opened the terrace windows, and laid the sunbonnet on the window sill. Thera appeared soon after with a big bucket of water, a mop, and cloths for drying. She worked quickly and efficiently and Lisa helped move the bed and heavy furniture so the girl could get at the years of dust beneath them. Finally she was finished and as she paused by the window to look out at the terrace she spied the sunbonnet. She went over to it at once and let her fingers move across it gently, lovingly. Lisa watched her.

"It will be a long, hot trip to Yialousa," Lisa said. "The mule cart is slow. Would you like to wear the bonnet?"

Thera's dark beauty erupted in an excited smile, the first real smile Lisa had ever seen on the girl's face, and she was once again struck by Thera's real loveliness. She was glad she had interfered that morning. Thera deserved much better than Kosta and his dour peasant ways.

"Oh, but I couldn't," Thera said, drawing back from the bonnet. "It was given to you to wear. It is yours."

"But I won't need it this morning," Lisa said. "And you're right, it is mine, and I can do what I want with it." She took the bonnet from the window sill and put it on Thera's black hair. "There now," she said. "Wear it for the trip. It's the middle of the morning and the sun is broiling now. Go on, get moving."

Thera's smile was pure delight as she skipped from the room, unmindful of the bucket and mop she carried. Lisa changed into slacks and a light green blouse and went downstairs in time to see Thera in the little two-wheeled cart, the mule starting to move off reluctantly. The bright yellow bonnet glistened in the sun and she heard Thera humming as the cart moved down the road. Turning, Lisa went into the dining hall where Maggie had a tableful of silver that had been exhumed from the storeroom.

"I told Thera to get some silver polish if she could, too," Maggie said. "Meanwhile, there's an awful lot of plain dirt and grime to get off these things as a start."

Lisa turned to Nikos and questioned the old man, having him repeat the unfamiliar words he used in answering her. Finally having the essence of what he'd said, she spoke to Maggie.

"If there's no polish available, Nikos says that pumice will do it," Lisa said. "I asked him what they used to use for silver and that's what he said." Maggie grimaced.

"Let's hope we can find some polish," she said. Lisa started to cart the largest pieces, big bowls and platters, into the kitchen to soak them in a tub of hot water. She was just beginning to attack the years of encrusted grime when she heard Maggie's yell and some very familiar Anglo-Saxon words that sounded almost welcome to her ears. She went out into the foyer to see Maggie standing by a small table holding up a leather drawstring purse.

"Dammit! She forgot the money," Maggie exclaimed in exasperation. "She was so excited about wearing that damned sunbonnet that she was walking on air. I had to remind her to take the three fixtures for size. And now she goes off without the money."

"That's a shame," Lisa said, feeling a little guilty.

"The whole trip a waste," Maggie growled. "The day a waste. That mule may not move very fast but even so you'd never catch up to her on foot. I wish I were one of those old Greek Olympic runners."

"Wait a moment," Lisa shouted. "My bicycle! I'd quite forgotten about it."

"Why, yes, you could catch her on that," Maggie chortled. She thrust the leather purse into Lisa's hand. "Well, don't just stand there, girl," she snapped. "Get a move on."

The cycle had been stored in the big kitchen pantry and it took but a moment to get it. The little purse tied around her wrist, she paused only to query Nikos about the road to Yialousa. There were two, he told her: one low by the shore, shorter but rougher with uneven terrain; the other in the hills, longer but smoother. "*Epharisto,*" Lisa said, though it was mere politeness. She hadn't learned a thing. Thera might have taken either road. Lisa decided on the lower one. It curved around behind Caramania, becoming not much more than a one-horse path for a while and then widening into the semblance of a road again. She came to a bearded old man seated at the edge of the road, putting fresh figs into small boxes of wood. He looked as though he had been there a long time and she skidded to a halt before him. At her questioning he told her he had indeed been there since sunup but he had seen no girl in a yellow bonnet driving a two-wheeled mule cart. Grimacing, Lisa doubled back at once and found the other road that swung up into the hills. She muttered a prayer of thanks to the years of practice the rugged hills of Vermont had given her. The sun blazed down and she was glad when the road leveled off and pedaling grew easier. She passed two old men walking and a farmer driving a wagon. The road cut through a hillside that sloped steeply to the right and as it twisted and turned, appearing and disappearing ahead, she peered forward to glimpse a flash of yellow. Rounding a tight curve she came onto a small straightaway and saw the yellow bonnet a distance away, on a curving portion of the road ahead, too far away to hail. She increased her speed, watching the yellow bonnet vanish around a curve and then reappear.

Suddenly she heard an unusual sound here in the hills of Cyprus—the roar of an automobile engine. She glanced behind as the car came around the curve. It was gray and old and not an American car; English or perhaps Italian, she guessed. The car roared toward her, going very fast, and she pulled to the edge of the road. The car shot past her and she glimpsed the driver, a dark-skinned man with a small moustasche and a black felt hat pulled low over his forehead. The car threw a cloud of dust at her and she bent her head to one side and closed her eyes. When she glanced up again the car was careening around the curve ahead. Moments later she wheeled around the bend and saw the yellow bonnet at the end of a straight stretch of road. The heavy, gray car was racing toward the little cart and Lisa, watching, saw it pull out to pass. It had come almost abreast of Thera when it suddenly turned sharply and smashed into the little cart. It was no sudden swerve but a deliberate turn, and Lisa saw the little cart upend and smash into splinters as the car drove it into the side of the hill. Thera's body and the yellow sunbonnet disappeared in the sickening sound of splintering wood. The car pushed the remains of the cart, no more than broken sticks of wood now, for a few added feet along the hillside and then veered out to roar away. It passed the little donkey who had pulled free of his harness at the first impact.

Lisa leaped from the bicycle as she reached the scene, running toward what had been the little cart. Thera lay against the side of the hill, amid the splintered wood, the sunbonnet a few feet away on the road. Lisa saw the trickle of red from her lips, saw the crushed, twisted contours of her body and she knew that Thera was dead. She sank down beside the girl's lifeless form and thought she was going to be sick. It wasn't waves of nausea that assailed her but waves of horror and anguish and she felt herself shocked to the point of numbness. She didn't remember getting to her feet, didn't remember picking up the sunbonnet, but she was standing with it in her hand, gazing down at Thera's crumpled form, when she heard the sound of loose rock falling down the hillside and she looked up. A shock of reddish hair bounced wildly in the sun as Michael scrambled down the steep slope, half falling the last few yards but somehow landing on his feet beside her. She felt his arms steadying her and she clung to him. There was a rocklike strength to his wide chest and his arms holding her were reassuringly comforting. She looked up at him, her lips trembling, and she was grateful that the usually mocking blue eyes were steady and grave.

"Did you see it?" she asked brokenly.

"No," he said. "I heard it. I was on my way to some old ruins on the top of these hills. When I looked down it was over but I could see the yellow bonnet. I wasn't sure it belonged to the figure getting off the bicycle or the one in the broken cart. Only when I got halfway down did I see it was you kneeling there."

His eyes were holding hers with deep concern and his hands pressed against her with something more than solace. Or was she just imagining that, she wondered fleetingly.

"Did you get anything to identify the car or the driver?" Michael asked.

"It was big and old and gray and I think an English car," Lisa said. "But it was no accident."

She saw Michael's eyes harden and his lips tighten. "You mean it was a hit-and-run. That's plain enough all right. I guess even here on Cyprus there are people who panic and become hit-and-run drivers."

She was going to say more but she held her tongue as the farmer drove up with the wagon. It could wait, and she had no stomach for Michael's skeptical logic. Not now. She looked away, the terrible numbness holding her in its grip as he spoke to the old farmer and told the man to hurry on to the nearest town and call the authorities. The man whipped his horse into a gallop and Michael steered her over to the other side of the road, found a flat rock, and had her sit down on it. She wanted to cry but she couldn't. The enormity of what had happened blotted out all else and she could see the heavy gray car before her as it smashed the little cart to bits and pieces. But she said nothing further yet though she knew once and for all, this time, what she had witnessed. Finally others came up the road, clinging to a small and ancient open truck. Michael spoke to them and she saw a blanket thrown over the lifeless form and then Michael, her bicycle in his hand, was standing beside her lifting her to her feet.

"Can you walk back?" he said. "Or do you want to wait for a wagon that's coming?"

"Let's walk," she said. "Yes, I want to walk." Walking seemed somehow more fitting and they started down the road, Michael wheeling the bicycle beside her. She walked in silence and he didn't intrude on her anguish. Not till they reached Orion Hall and he put the cycle in the foyer did he speak to her.

"Lisa," he said. "Tell me what I can do for you." Lisa turned to him and felt the rush of anger and bitterness seize her. "You could try believing me for a change," she said, deep pain shouldering anger in her eyes. Maggie took that moment to appear and Michael quickly told her what had happened. Maggie listened in silence and when he'd finished her eyes swept them both.

Michael hesitated and then spoke again. "Lisa doesn't think it was an accident," he said tightly.

"I know it was no accident," Lisa said, her voice cold, flat. "The car drove up to the cart, turned, and crashed directly into it."

"Lisa," Michael said and she saw that he was trying to be gentle, his eyes holding hers steadily. "It may have looked that way. It may even have happened that way. But any car suddenly swerving out of control would look much the same. Until the driver is found you can't say things like that; you can't read murder into everything."

"That's the right word," Lisa said, feeling a steely determination rising inside her. This wasn't the stuff of legends or dark imaginings but deliberate murder in the bright sun of the day.

"Why do you think it was done on purpose?" Maggie's voice cut in.

"Because I was the one the driver was out to kill," she said.

"You mean he missed you and hit the cart instead?" Maggie asked.

"No," Lisa shot back. "Thera was wearing this." She held out the sunbonnet. "Whoever it was thought I was driving that little cart. I'm supposed to be the girl dead back there on that road. He crashed into her deliberately, thinking it was me."

Her eyes were holding Maggie's now and she saw the grim fear on the older woman's face. "You can't be sure," Maggie said. "You don't have any proof whatever that you're right about this or about any of the other things that have happened and which you interpreted the same way."

"What things?" Michael asked and Lisa stood by silently as Maggie recited the girl's fears that a person or persons was try-ing to keep her aunt from living at Orion Hall. Maggie was fair, leaving out nothing, starting with the crude, anonymous letters and the little lawyer. Maggie, of course, didn't know about the man, Kosta, outside the hotel room. But as she recounted each thing, Lisa realized how each one separately could be so easily explained away, as easily as Michael's "psychic hallucinations" had explained away her brush with death at the bottom of the seawall that night. Maggie didn't know about that, of course, nor did she know the true story of the legend of Athena. And Lisa wasn't about to add those at this time.

When Maggie finished, Lisa answered simply: "Put all those things together and you can't explain them away. And today I was there. I know what I saw." She held up the yellow bonnet. "This was the mark of death," she said. "It's pure logic to me."

"Then it ought to be pure logic to suspect your friend Demetrius," Michael snapped. "After all, he gave the bonnet to you."

Lisa felt her temper explode with an almost unreasonable fury. "What a rotten, stinking thing to say," she shot out. "Yes, he gave it to me but the whole town knew I had it. Any number of people could have seen me with it. Anyone watching me would have seen it. I wore it all day with Demetrius yesterday. And I had it on when I met you at the quay in the afternoon."

Michael merely shrugged. "Besides," Lisa added, "that would have been a rather transparent device, I'd say."

"Maybe," Michael said dryly. "But effective."

Lisa's eyes shot daggers at him and he held his cool glance. "I was only following through on your suppositions," he smiled thinly.

"It doesn't really matter," Maggie cut in. "Lisa is right in that any number of people could have seen her in the bonnet. But that still doesn't make her suspicions right about the accident being deliberate. And, in any case, I can't leave here and that's that."

Abruptly, without another word or glance, Maggie turned and went up the stairway, her steps slow and her body reflecting her inner weariness. Lisa, watching her go, vowed to clear up that cryptic statement before the day ended. She felt Michael's hand on her arm, turning her to him.

"Look, I've been thinking about this," he said. "You're apparently addicted to close calls."

"More than you know," she said tartly and saw him frown.

"I went into the east turret last night," she said.

"You what?" he half shouted.

"I went into the east turret, all the way to the very top," she said. "I found out how Athena fell from it on that night the legend was born."

As Michael listened with a deepening frown she told him what had happened and how the loose stone had almost pitched her to her death also. When she finished there was shock and anger in his eyes.

"You know, you ought not to be left alone," he said. "You're a positive menace to yourself and that's all the more reason I want you to leave here, leave Cyprus, leave this blasted old gargoyle of a house."

"You too?" she said in surprise.

"Someone else tell you you should leave?"

"Demetrius," Lisa said, once more hearing the smugness in her voice. "He wants both Maggie and me to go but you just heard Maggie on that. He doesn't have explanations, either, but he feels that old legends have a way of causing new troubles and he wants me safely out of here."

"How nice," Michael mused aloud. "My reasons don't touch on witches and old spells and ghostly spirits."

"I know," Lisa cut in, her tone acid. "That's all just psychic hallucination. But I haven't heard you coming up with any logical explanations for what I've seen and felt and been terrified of inside me. Pomegranates and terrace steps, explain them to me. I'm still waiting."

She saw his lips tighten and his eyes flash for an instant. "I can't," he said quietly. "But I know why you should leave here."

"Why?" Lisa asked curtly.

"Behavioral probabilities and statistical conclusions make it important," Michael said, his eyes once again cool and contained. "First of all, you have those suspicions about someone trying to keep your aunt from living here. Then you're uptight about the legend of Athena and how it touches you. Those two things lead you into danger-oriented situations and will keep on doing so. You're all caught up in it and you'll keep on mucking about to find out more. Your imagination and your suspicions will keep you at it. Those are the behavioral probabilities. Statistically you've been very lucky but also, again statistically, your luck is bound to run out. Then you'll get yourself killed. If you're safely away from here you won't be endangering yourself."

"You make it all sound so tender and touching," Lisa said waspishly.

"Maybe your friend Demetrius' romantic concern for you and legends is more appealing," Michael said dryly. "Mine makes more sense."

"At least he doesn't scoff and disbelieve the things I tell him and that's important."

"I don't swallow things without questioning and that's important."

"He's concerned for my feelings."

"I'm concerned for your neck."

Lisa held his blue eyes with her gaze and suddenly she felt somewhat unworthy. After all, he had saved her life and he could be sensitive once in a while. "I'm sorry," she said. "Did you mean what you just said, about being concerned, I mean?"

"Certainly," he said. "You're fascinating." His eyes were steady, serious, and then his face broke into that wide insouciant grin. "Anybody who goes in all directions at once is fascinating," he tossed at her and slipped out the door as she felt her temper skyrocketing. He could hold out something sweet with one hand and whisk it away with the other. It was certainly a talent of sorts. And not one she needed, she told herself angrily. She started for Maggie's room, realizing once again that despite what she felt so certain of, she had to have more time to sort out things and find unrefutable evidence. Once more she had seen how everything that had happened could be explained away but now there was something else on her mind, something she could get cleared up. Maggie was sitting on the edge of the high-backed chair by the window, her face lined, her eyes sad. Lisa touched the older woman's shoulder gently.

"Why can't you leave here with me, Maggie?" she asked. "Why did you say that?"

She saw Maggie's chin lift in pride, that commanding presence of hers fighting its way to the surface.

"Because, my dear, I am, for all serious purposes, without income," she said simply. "Except for a few paltry dollars I receive from some annuities, I am what is generally referred to as 'broke.'"

Maggie smiled at the frown of disbelief that crossed Lisa's face and she patted the girl's arm. "It's my own fault," she said. "I never paid proper attention to finances, to investments. Companies my father had bought stock in for me went broke. Property I could have sold went down in value till it was practically worthless. I paid no attention to advice from my investment counselors. And I made a few foolish investments on my own until suddenly the day came when it was clear I would soon be financially wrecked. Certainly I hadn't enough to live the good life in England anymore. I started to cast about desperately and came upon the papers for Orion Hall. It was a solution for me, my only solution, really. No rent, a cost of living low enough for me to afford, and quiet and beauty. In time some of my holdings will go back up in value, but not for quite a while. Meanwhile Orion Hall was here, the perfect place for me and perhaps the last stop for me. My remaining funds have been deposited in a bank in Kyrenia by now. My bank in Sussex was transferring them. With them and my small income I can make this place very livable."

Lisa said nothing but some of the past remarks Maggie had made now made sense.

"So you see, Lisa, my dear," Maggie continued, "there's no place for me to go. And even if your worst suspicions should be right, I'm staying. Perhaps a show of determination is all that's really necessary."

Lisa winced inwardly. Once she might have gone along with that. Now the sense of danger, that damned spirit of evil again, was too much with her. But Maggie's next words fell on ears both deaf and determined.

"Perhaps you ought to get away from here, Lisa," the older woman said. "Nikos manages to understand my sign language pretty well and I'll just have to concentrate on picking up Greek faster."

"Oh, no," Lisa said. "I'm not one for running out on people. I'm staying until we get to the bottom of this."

She wanted to say more but there were voices from down-stairs and she hurried down to see Nikos talking to three men in dark suits. They greeted Lisa and showed their credentials. They were from the police at Yialousa and they took down her story as she reported it. The car had been found, they told her, abandoned outside of Yialousa. It was an unregistered car with no record of ownership or even of its existence on Cyprus.

"Sometimes people smuggle in vehicles in the night at lonely coastal spots," one officer told Lisa. "This was no doubt one of them."

It was, in short, a blank wall, Lisa saw. The men expressed their sorrow at what had happened and promised a continued hunt for the driver of the car. Perhaps someone would come forward with information. It was always a possibility. Lisa thanked them for their efforts and watched them leave. When they'd gone she went into the kitchen and made some coffee for herself. She took the cup up to her room and sipped the strong, warm liquid as she sorted things out in her mind. Was it really important that they had tried to kill her and killed Thera instead, she asked herself. Was this all really so removed from legends and dark curses? If evil was indeed a real force, could she not be touched by it? Every day scientists discover how little they know about the wonders of inherited characteristics. Knowledge, once believed to be strictly in the area of acquired intelligence, was now viewed as possibly transmittable. Experiments with flatworms had proven the hereditary transmission of certain learned abilities. Could not unfathomed arrangements of chromosomes carry the stain of evil, carry it as certainly as any other seed? Was there, inside her, such a Cimmerian presence that had lain dormant and needed only the right combination of time and place to make itself known? Was she touched by the evil of Athena, an evil that the dark turbulence of Cyprus had nourished into flower? Had her very presence here brought all this down on the heads of the innocent? Had her coming unleashed the dark forces that had silently waited? If so, she should leave at once. Maggie would be better off without her presence. Even if it had been the hatred of the man, Kosta, behind the latest attempt on her life, it was her being there that had caused that hatred.

But that didn't explain the unseen blow that had struck her that night by the seawall. And what if there really were no plot to keep Maggie from living here? What if all that had happened had been accidental and coincidental? Lisa turned and went out of the room, hurrying down the stairs. If there were answers she would have to clear her mind somehow to find a way to discard the unreal. But how could you discard what was unreal merely because it had no rational explanation? Her mind was too full of dark fears for her to marshal her thoughts. She wanted to talk to someone, to Demetrius, someone with understanding and sympathy. Perhaps it would clear her mind, or at least calm her tossing turbulence so she could think clearly. She walked quickly, remembering that Demetrius had said he would be back from Kyrenia by the afternoon and the afternoon was far along now. She strode through the narrow streets, past the market square, down to the quay, and then back up again. She was about to turn to go back to Orion Hall when she saw him, just leaving one of the whitewashed houses, and she called to him. He whirled and stared at her, shocked disbelief in his eyes. She ran toward him as he stood transfixed and then he cried out and swung her up in his arms.

"You are alive!" he exclaimed. "I could not believe my eyes it was really you. They had told me of the accident on the road to Yialousa and of the girl who was killed. She had worn a yellow sunbonnet, they said."

"It was Thera," Lisa said. "I'd given her the bonnet to wear."

Demetrius was holding her by the waist, frowning down at her. "I did not go to your aunt when I heard about it," he said. "I was too crushed to talk to her, to anyone. And now here you are, unharmed, alive."

He hugged her to him and she was glad for the warm strength of his arms, the magnificent power of his hands. "Come, we will stop at the cafe for a little wine," he said. "I shall have brandy. I can use the drink."

At the cafe by the quay Lisa told him of the accident and how the car had roared past her to deliberately smash into Thera. She also told him Maggie refused to leave, though she didn't feel it proper to go into why Maggie refused. She was going to tell him about her visit to the east turret but he clasped her hands in his warm, strong grip when she spoke of Maggie.

"Then we must find other plans for your safety," he said. "At least till your aunt changes her mind. I am deeply bothered by the strange things you have seen and felt, the things you have told me about. There are things which surpass our understanding, certainly mine. But sometimes there are signs for us to follow. I want you to stay close to the house and be patient. Perhaps a sign will come to you, something will happen that will make you see which way to go."

Lisa nodded and thought of how she had had to go into the east tower, how an invisible force had pulled her there. "I am going to keep checking on this business with the car today," Demetrius said. "And I shall look into the actions of this fellow Kosta for you. Meanwhile I want you to just be calm and not do anything foolish. It will all work out, you wait and see. Something will happen that will shed light on all of this. I have confidence in the good things."

He stood up, pulling her with him, and they walked slowly back to the dark door of Orion Hall. He left her with a brush of his lips and walked on. She saw his handsome face grow tight as he walked off and his jaw muscles twitched and he seemed another man, someone with a great many things to do and do quickly. She went upstairs, thinking of how shocked he had been at seeing her, and how wonderfully warm and understanding afterwards. Of course, Michael had said he had her interests at heart, too, but she wondered if this were really so. Michael had tossed the left-handed accusation at Demetrius when she had spoken of the sunbonnet. Had he done so to shake her confidence in Demetrius, to give her no place to turn but himself? Was it a kind of jealousy, or something much more, much deadlier? He had appeared very conveniently nearby the scene of the tragedy this morning, she recalled. Had he really been there waiting, watching? His eyes, too, had been shocked when he saw her standing beside the crumpled form in the yellow bonnet. Two men, both professing concern for her. Two pairs of eyes, both shocked at seeing her alive. Was one of them lying? She gazed out the window of her room at the curved slash of a moon that hung in the sky. Her eyes swept over the terrace steps. No matter what else there was, the legend of Athena was still there, deep inside her. There could be no fleeing this house now, not until her tortured fears were satisfied. Perhaps the unexplained was destined to remain so for always. But somehow, some way, she would have to try. Somehow, some way, she would have to meet the unknown or she would live a life damned to wonder and doomed to fear. Cyprus, land of a thousand secrets and ten thousand legends, held one marked for her. That Lisa Bowen knew in her heart as she undressed and lay down to sleep.

CHAPTER SEVEN

"So long as he has a tooth left a fox won't be pious."
—CYPRIOTE GREEK PROVERB.

A KIND OF FATALISTIC RESIGNATION possessed her when she got up in the morning, coupled with a dogged determination. It was as though she had embarked on a course from which there was no turning back and in so doing experienced a sense of inner relief. Maggie had gone to see about burial arrangements for Thera and Lisa was grateful to her aunt for taking on the somber task. She had no stomach for it and she continued to feel a terrible responsibility for Thera's death. The girl had no relatives anyone knew of in all of Caramania and the village officials agreed to do all the things necessary and proper for a funeral in the Greek Orthodox faith. It was that afternoon, after Maggie had returned, that Lisa met both Demetrius and Michael in town. Demetrius was first and she saw him as she went into Caramania with Nikos to shop at the market. He was just emerging from the whitewashed building she had seen him leaving the day before and she called out to him. He waited beside the doorway of the small two-story house as she came up to him.

"Is this where you live when you're in Caramania?" Lisa asked. Demetrius nodded and his hand found her waist for a moment.

"I would have liked to bring you here," he said, his face serious. "But to do so, to bring you, a single girl, to my place, would cause much talk here in a village such as Caramania. It would not be good for you."

"Of course," Lisa smiled at him. "I understand."

"But if you ever need me, this is my place here," Demetrius said. "Do not hesitate to come here if you are in trouble."

Lisa nodded and nodded again as he made her promise to stay close to Orion Hall, to stay within its protective walls and bide her time. "I may have to go away tomorrow for the day," Demetrius said. "But I'll be back the next day and come to see you."

"Promise?" she laughed and he nodded, his handsome face serious and even handsomer because of it. There was no more talk of her leaving Orion Hall as there had been the day before. There were only his warm words. "I will watch out for you, Lisa," he said to her. "Do not be afraid."

It was later, after she and Nikos had returned to the great house, that she met Michael. She was outside the main door bringing in some kindling wood from along the side of the house when he came down the road that ran from the hills behind into the village. His blue eyes surveyed her, taking in her figure as if she were standing there without clothes, and she felt her temper rise at once. She glared at him.

"Just jogging the memory," he grinned at her and then his face grew serious, abruptly, startlingly. "I hope you've decided to get out of here as I told you to," he said.

"I'm staying," Lisa said. "Until Maggie's able to handle things herself."

She saw the line of his jaw harden but he kept the cool self-assurance in his eyes.

"I suppose a sensible decision would have been too much to expect of you," he said, his eyes narrowed.

"I suppose so," she snapped back. "You can't expect common sense from people who go about seeing things, can you?"

It was his turn to glare at her and for a moment she was happy to see that he lost the cool, contained control in his eyes. Flashing a brief smile at him, she turned and went into the house with the kindling. He had been angered, that was plain. Even his cool facade couldn't hide that. Was it because every effort to get her away from Orion Hall had failed? Or had more than that failed? It was hard to think of Michael as involved in any plot. His sarcastic tongue could be infuriating. His self-assured, cool manner was provoking. But his broad, pleasant face was, while not handsome, certainly attractive and his eyes could sparkle with warmth as well as cynicism. There was just nothing menacing about him and yet she had once heard that some of the most deadly killers had the faces of angels. She could not take risks on outward appearances, not here where almost every outward sign masked something else. Death walked this island, lurked in the shadows of night and in the innocence of the sunlit mornings. It wore a mask, perhaps many masks. It would strike again, she knew, though she didn't know how soon. She put the kindling wood beside the big fireplace in the dining hall and helped Maggie finish fixing dinner. The old man ate with them and Lisa led a small Greek lesson for Maggie. Dinner took its leisurely course and by the time they had finished cleaning up, Maggie was ready for bed. The somber tasks of the burial negotiations had drained her spirit and Lisa, too, felt tired and depressed. In her room she watched the embers of a small fire she made die away and then went to bed sleep enveloping her almost at once.

Only a few hours had passed when she woke, sitting up in the large bed. She heard the sound of the big oaken front door creak open, once, then again. Putting a loose shift over her nightgown she stepped into her slippers, took the kerosene lamp from the dresser, and went into the corridor. She didn't light the lamp, holding it in front of her more as a weapon. As she stepped into the corridor she heard the sound of her slipper slap against the stone and she lifted her foot to see that the sole had come loose. There would be nothing silent about her movements with that flapping about, she knew, and she stepped out of the slippers, leaving them in front of her door. Barefoot, she moved down the corridor, pausing at the head of the stairs, listening. There was no sound from the blackness below. Slowly, soft as a cat, she crept down the wide stairs, pausing with each step to listen. But there was no other sound and soon she was at the bottom of the stairs. She went to the big door. It was closed, the bolt on from the inside, and she frowned. Had she imagined the sound of it being opened? Or had Nikos perhaps gotten up and closed it? She hadn't remembered bolting it. In fact, she didn't recall their ever bolting the front door shut since they'd been at Orion Hall.

Lisa turned and went back up the stairs, again moving carefully and pausing to listen every few steps. But the house was silent and she walked back to her room. She stopped before her slippers, lifted her foot to step into them, then drew back. They were together, just as she'd left them, but they hadn't been that close to the wall. She stepped back further and reached out with the lamp, using the edge of it to catch the heel of the left slipper. She flipped it over and drew back quickly. The slipper lay there on its side and her frown deepened. Moving carefully, Lisa reached out with the edge of the lamp again until she touched the other slipper. Kneeling on one knee to steady herself, she pushed it over. She jumped back involuntarily as the wicked-looking little creature scurried from inside the slipper, its long, whiplike body curved up over itself. It was a scorpion, she recognized at once, its deadly stinging tail upraised, ready to strike. The creature scurried a few feet away and paused. Lisa picked up the slipper. She couldn't let it scurry off to some crevice to strike unexpectedly some other time. The slipper in her hand, she moved toward the deadly little creature. The scorpion backed off, sensing danger, ready to strike. But the danger fell on it from above as Lisa came down with all her might with the slipper. She didn't need to look. The deadly creature lay dead under the slipper and she turned and fled into her room. She stood by the bed, trembling. Once again it would have been one of those things, a tragic accident. The scorpion could have crawled into her slipper while she was downstairs. Death wore its clever mask once more and only she knew the deadly creature had been placed in her slipper to wait there in the darkness of it for her to step into.

Whoever had put it there had already fled the house, Lisa knew as she sank down on the bed. It would not be hard to enter and leave the great house unseen, through the front door, bolting it afterwards, or perhaps through the stables or a window. The killer had no doubt intended to plant the scorpion in some spot, perhaps on her as she lay asleep. The slippers in front of her door were an unexpected dividend for him. And had she not noticed they'd been moved ever so slightly, it would have worked. The killing venom would have done its work in her bloodstream, a tragic *accidental* ocurrence.

But who had done it, Lisa asked the four walls. Someone who knew his way around Orion Hall. But then who in Caramania did not? The great house had stood empty so long that many no doubt had visited it. Or perhaps, as she thought of its history, perhaps not so many. Kosta might well know every nook and cranny, though, and his vengeance was still unsatisfied. And Michael had admitted he had visited Orion Hall. As she thought more about it, the years of study of Greek history and drama welled up in her mind, lighting almost forgotten darkness. The use of the scorpion to kill her had its own meaning as well as being diabolically clever. In Greek mythology Orion had been the greatest of all hunters, but his very skill and prowess had made him vain and boastful. He told Diana, Goddess of the Hunt, that he would kill every animal on earth. Diana sent a scorpion to Orion which stung him to death with its fatal venom.

Lisa almost smiled. Orion Hall and death by a scorpion, echoes of ancient Greek mythology. Whoever had thought of using the scorpion knew the mythology of ancient Greece and had a sense of irony. Did that narrow down the suspects, she wondered. Kosta was but a rough peasant, certainly no student of ancient history. And yet she was more than certain that even the humblest peasant here knew the legends and mythology of his heritage. And of course there was Michael Barry. He would certainly know it. So would Demetrius, but she didn't even linger on his name, save for a moment of warmth. No, the knowledge of it did not really help. And it might have been someone completely unknown to her. But the killer had tried again, in but another variation of the same clever manner. This had been something out of the past, something of the stuff of legends, yet also cold, clever, attempted murder and suddenly a thought struck the girl with such force it was almost a physical blow. Perhaps she had been thinking incorrectly all the time, perhaps there was no either/or answer. Perhaps the legend of Athena and the hold the past had on her was but one of two very different things going on here on this island. Perhaps pomegranates and terrace steps and strange visions in the night were something entirely separate from these cold-blooded killings and attempted killings. Had they just come together here and now in an evil conjuncture? Lisa lay down and pulled the sheet over her long, slender form. Demetrius had been right. She would have to bide her time and wait for some sign. Everything else was only questions that brought more questions. That and the certainty that death searched for her in this great house, on this island of deceptions, as surely as a fox hunts for the hare. What face would it finally have when the time for unmasking came? A face torn out of the past, out of the deep darkness of her own blood heritage? Or a face from the cold sinistemess of today?

She turned over and let sleep fight off any further thoughts.

CHAPTER EIGHT

"By suffering, comes wisdom."
—AESCHYLUS

THE MORNING DAWNED with the sun barely burning its way
through a blue-gray haze. Lisa stared out the window at the
mist that blanketed the scene. She wondered if by night it would
turn to fog and a sudden excitement swept over her, though she
didn't know why. After dressing in blue jeans and an old shirt
she went downstairs, having already made up her mind to say
nothing of the scorpion and the slippers. She paused outside the
door to pick up the old slippers and the grisly remains beneath
one and toss them into the big garbage can back of the kitchen.
The day had been planned for her to work with Nikos, cementing
breaks and cracks in the north wall of the stable. The donkey had
been returned and Nikos said he would find a new cart soon. As
she worked on the wide gaps of the wall with the old man she
again realized how easy it had been for someone to enter Orion
Hall during the night.

But the work was satisfyingly hard and kept her body and
her mind busy on doing a good job. It made the day go swiftly
and after dinner with Maggie and Nikos again, and another
Greek lesson over dessert, Lisa was happy to see the day come
to an end. She went to her room tired, anxious to turn in early.
Before falling into bed she went to the window and looked out

onto the terrace. The day's haze had turned to thick fog that curled itself around the great house, painting the night with an opaque brush, promising to grow still heavier as the night grew older. The strange excitement she had felt on seeing the haze in the morning returned to race through her body as though the fog carried its own promise, though she knew not of what. She could feel it, smell its dampness as it filtered through cracks and spaces in the old window frames and the door. Finally the girl turned from the window and crept into the warmth of the big bed, lying awake for some while before sleep wrapped itself around her. She slept fitfully, tossing and turning, and the hours ticked on until the dark had just turned the corner of midnight and the girl woke, her eyes snapping open in the blackness.

The sound rose up in the night, faint but insistent, the eerie, bone-chilling sound she had come to know. It echoed up to the room, wafting through the fog, a long, singsong wail, like a scream that had tried to become a cry or a cry that had tried to become a laugh. Lisa swung her long, slender legs from the bed and wondered if the cold that gripped her came from the damp of the room or the dark of her soul. She went to the window and peered through the fog that swirled and blew in long gray ribbons. Her eyes burned as she tried to pierce the curtained night, to see down to the bottom terrace. And then, as she peered, a breath of wind came and the tendrils of fog parted, a moment's tear in the curtain. Lisa gasped. It was there, the black-robed figure, by the wall of the bottom terrace. The wailing grew in pitch and then fell away and the figure moved, or seemed to move. It was hard to tell as the fog closed in, swept by, revealing then concealing.

Lisa turned and threw slacks and a dark sweater on, moving with unhurried speed. She knew what she would do, what she must do, as though some unheard voice had spoken to her. There would be no going down through the house and out to the seawall this time. That way was to risk another unseen blow in the blanketing fog. Going down the terrace steps she could not be attacked from behind. But could she go down them? Her heart began to pound at the mere thought. But below, on the last terrace, there was an answer waiting, an answer she must have, an answer she so desperately wanted. Lisa paused by the dresser, pulled open the drawer, and took out the jade ring. She slipped it on her finger, took one of the heavy andirons from beside the fireplace, and opened the door to the terrace. She ran out into the fog, hardly able to see her hands in front of her, but she found the terrace steps as the wind lightened the heavy vapors.

Lisa saw the first of the steps and started toward them. At once the nausea began to well up inside her, choking, sickening, a fear like no fear she had ever known. Tensing her muscles she began to run, racing with her breath harsh, her blood pounding in her temples. She ran, increasing her speed, and flung herself past the first step, her feet barely touching the second to land on the third. A terrible shuddering blow struck her, only it was a blow from within, and she felt bands of ice tightening around her chest, crushing, suffocating. Invisible hands seemed to pull her back but she fought desperately against a force unseen, pulling herself from the wall where she had stopped, forcing her steps downward. Her body was bathed in perspiration and her breasts hurt her as breathing became a burning, choking sensation. But she kept going, down, down another step, and then another. She walked in a column of air that was not merely cold but clammy with some remembered death. Her feet were leaden and a terrible weight pulled at her every step. It was, and she swallowed with difficulty, as though she were dragging something behind her. Her fearful glance backwards revealed only the fog and she stumbled forward, suddenly finding her feet on the level of the second terrace.

Lisa halted and leaned against the wall, using it to make her way toward the flight of steps leading to the last terrace. She did so, the fog below swirled away for a moment, and she saw the ghostly white triangle below. It moved, and her eyes focused on it It was the sail of a fishing dory and through another moment's gap in the fog she saw a second one. Again her ears picked up the sound of rowing, of oars creaking in rowlocks. The dories moved near to the shore, heading close by the village quay, and then the fog closed in again. The sails vanished, as ghostly as they had appeared. But Lisa knew they had been real. Or she thought she knew. She plunged on, down the last flight of terrace steps, and now the coldness around her was less so, the bands of ice around her chest less tight. But she still had the invisible weight at her back and she paused to wipe the hand that clutched the andiron. The wails were louder now and the fog that closed in on her was both thick and vaporous. As she made her way forward the fog tore apart briefly and she saw she was almost down to the last terrace. Lisa gasped. The figure was still there, by the seawall, tall, robed in black. It vanished for a moment and then reappeared, turning toward her. A black hood covered the head and no face could be seen within the depths of the cowl. The figure moved toward her and Lisa glimpsed a white garment beneath the long black robe. She thought she heard other sounds in the fogbound night but she couldn't be certain—voices, the sound of rowing—the wailing filled the air and played tricks with all else. Lisa saw the figure come toward her through the mist, arms outstretched, and she shrank back. What was this fearsome thing, this black-robed wraith? Was this her destiny, to face this apparition, this cloaked and hooded spirit? Had terrible, unfathomable powers out of the past called her back here to Orion Hall to complete a strange cycle of death?

The figure was more hidden than seen now in the swirling fog. All Lisa could make out was the tall, shrouded form moving toward her, arms outstretched, reaching for her. The figure half vanished and then came through the curtained blanket of air. Lisa raised the andiron clutched in her hand. Terror lending new strength to her, she swung the heavy andiron in a wide arc and felt it strike something solid. A harsh gutteral cry sounded in the fog, almost an animal sound. The blow had seemingly released the terror inside her and now the girl swung again and again, fury and desperation and terror exploding within. She felt the second blow strike something again and the hooded shape disappeared in the fog but Lisa kept swinging the andiron, flailing at the fog in all directions, remembering the unseen blow that had once struck her from behind. She moved back, putting the terrace wall against her, and kept sweeping the night with the powerful andiron.

She heard sounds of movement in the obscured and impenetrable darkness but mostly she heard the wailing and the sound of her own voice, sobbing and gasping as she kept swinging her weapon at the air. Finally, her arms about to fall off with fatigue, she turned and ran back up the terrace steps. On the top step she whirled, the andiron poised, waiting for the shrouded shape to materialize in pursuit. But there was nothing and she ran again, back into the house, bolting the door behind her. She let the andiron fall from her hand with a clatter and threw herself onto the bed, her body heaving with deep, gasping breaths, her skin cold with perspiration. But inside her, she felt more than she could grasp. She had faced something and she knew not what. But she had faced it, whatever it was. Had she faced the call of death and won? Had she faced something risen from the past and triumphed? She wanted desperately to tell herself it was so and yet the pieces didn't quite fit; there were things as unclear and foggy as the night. She heard the wailing, calling, crying sound stop and her breath returned to normal. She lay there and fell asleep, knowing only that she had gone down to the terrace and that she was still alive and that there was more to know, much more.

The day found her on the bed where she'd thrown herself, still dressed in the slacks and sweater, the andiron on the floor beside her. Lisa opened her eyes and something on her hand glinted. She focused on the jade and the coiled serpent of the ring on her finger. She sat up, ran her other hand over it, and then slipped it from her finger and put it back in the dresser. She picked up the andiron and put it back in its place. The touch of its cold iron reminded her again that she had fallen asleep on a triumph that refused to be a triumph. She had faced the dark forces of the past and there had been a false note in the siren song. The ethereal had been very real, the shadow had had substance. She looked down at the andiron again. It had been no wraith that iron had struck in the fog, no ghostly spirit, but something solid. Twice she had felt her blows strike solidly before the shrouded form had vanished in the fogbound night. She had struck out at the night, at the air, but not before her blows had struck something else.

Lisa flung open the terrace door and ran across the stones to the steps. She ran down the terrace steps and there were no cold bands around her chest, no weight dragging behind her. She felt excitement but not fear and nausea. That much she had met and conquered, she knew, that victory was hers and hers alone. In the morning sun the bottom terrace was clear and inviting. She put her back against the wall of the terrace and she swung an imaginary andiron in the air. Now her arms held the invisible andiron outstretched and her eyes dropped down to the stones of the terrace at the spot where the blows had struck during the night. A dark red spot stained the stone and Lisa knelt down at once. There was another a foot away, then two more, forming a trail to the short flight of steps that led from the terrace down to the seawall and the shoreline. She drew her finger across the stain and looked at the still fresh redness of it. Blood, unmistakably blood. Lisa's eyes narrowed. Whatever other dark forces existed here, the black-robed figure of Athena that had prowled the terrace last night was no ghostly spirit.

But what did it all mean, she asked herself, and knew that the answers still eluded her. She peered out into the sea waters where she had seen the two ghostly sails. They had been sailing close to shore, too close for normal travel. Just beyond the village quay the basalt cliffs rose up sharply from the water's edge. That bore further investigation and she felt a new excitement coursing through her body. But this time she would say nothing to anyone of what she'd found so far. No, this time she would make no accusations that could be glibly explained away. This time she would pursue things until she had evidence gathered to prove her suspicions. She started to turn to go back up the terrace steps when a rowboat rounded the corner of the seawall and she paused to look down at it. The figure in it waved casually at her and brushed back an unruly shock of reddish hair. He pointed the rowboat at the shoreline just beyond the wall of the terrace and Lisa went down the small flight of steps that led to the ground. She stood there as he nosed the rowboat onto the shore and all she could think of was the sound of oars she had heard in the night, last night and that other time when she was struck from behind at this very spot.

"I didn't know you had a rowboat," Lisa said coolly.

"Sure, keep it back of the cottage," Michael answered. "I try to row some every day. Good exercise."

His glance at her was thoughtful and his blue eyes were grave, with a tenderness in them she saw but didn't really believe she saw.

"I was worried about you last night," he said. "I hardly slept because of it."

Lisa felt her lips tighten. His voice held a new note of tenderness, too. Or he was a damned good actor.

"Why did you worry about me last night?" she asked, holding onto her cool poise.

"I saw the fog and I wondered if something might happen to make you risk your neck again," he said. "I know your type and it could well have happened. I started to walk over here a couple of times but the fog was so thick I couldn't make it. Walked into the ocean twice before I gave up."

Lisa wanted to trust Michael but she had learned that trust was a dangerous commodity here.

"As you can see I'm here and quite well," she said. "So that proves your worries were unfounded. Though I suppose I should thank you for worrying."

Michael's eyes were studying her speculatively. "That proves not a damn thing," he said slowly. "You could have just had another run of luck."

If he were trying to trap her into finding out how much or how little she'd learned she wouldn't fall for it, Lisa warned herself.

"I guess so," she said coolly. "But in any case I'm a big girl. I can take care of myself."

"I wish I could believe that, Lisa," he said, but there was no bite to his voice. There was only an unexpected gentleness. "See that you do, won't you?" he added and she felt sorry she'd been so tart with him. Damn him, he could be nice but always when you didn't expect it or even want it. She had started to turn away and paused. But the suddenness of his appearance after Thera's murder, his anger when she refused to leave after he'd told her to go, his skeptical rejection of her accounts, and now the rowboat, all came up to stick in her throat. No, she had to keep her distrust, to guard it as she would a shield. Conscious of his eyes watching her she went up the steps to the lowest terrace and then up the others. Halfway up she looked down. He was still watching her. She waved and continued on.

Once in her room she bathed, changed her clothes, and put on a pair of blue jeans and an old shirt, and hurried downstairs. Maggie was breakfasting already and planning tasks for everyone. Lisa was assigned to continue helping Nikos cement the stable walls. It suited her fine. It was hard, physical work but it would free her mind to make plans of her own that were already loosely forming in her head. By the time the day was half over she knew just what she would do first and she waited excitedly for the night. When it finally came she was glad to see it was clear but dark, with a moon so new in the sky it was but a thin curve of a line. She lay awake in the dark of her room until she was certain Maggie and the old man were both sound asleep. Then she rose quietly and began to change clothes.

Minutes later another kind of wraith appeared on the terrace to make its way down the steps, a creature of loveliness, of long, bare legs and bare torso moving swiftly, silently. She would have preferred a one-piece suit for this but bikinis were all she had in her suitcase. No matter, she didn't expect an audience. At the bottom of the last short flight of steps she turned and followed the line of the outside wall of the terrace to the sea. The swim would not cause her trouble. She had always excelled in swimming and she would pace herself. Once more she thought of ghostly spirits that could bleed and wails in the night and boats and sails that crept through the fog near shore. It all added up to something and perhaps the answer lay amid the steep sides of the basalt cliffs beyond the village quay. She was going to see, at least. Lisa stepped into the water and in moments she was swimming slowly, easily, in even, steady strokes, leaving the towering outline of the great house and following the line of the shore.

She soon passed the silent, sleeping village with its short waterfront, hardly longer than the quay itself, and continued on, hugging the shoreline. The sharp stone cliffs began to rise up almost immediately once she passed the end of the village and she slowed her pace, pausing to tread water and look up at the scrub brush and foliage that partially covered the stone cliffs. It grew more profuse along the bottom of the cliffs where it drew nourishment from the water. Every so often she turned to go directly to the rocky shoreline to investigate a shadowed indentation, a particularly dark crevice. But she found nothing that could accommodate rowboats, let alone sailing dories. Intent on her searching she never looked back or she might have seen the rowboat that followed her, keeping far behind. It had followed her from the moment she lowered herself into the water beneath the shadow of Orion Hall.

Becoming discouraged, Lisa nevertheless swam on, her eyes beginning to burn from the effort of peering through the darkness at the shadowed formations of the cliffs. There was no graded shoreline here, only the steep cliffs which came down to meet the deep water. A boat could certainly hug these shores without fear of running aground, she mused. But her arms were beginning to tire and she had to save her strength for the swim back. She was about to turn, bitterly disappointed but realizing now that it had been perhaps a piece of foolishness on her part. The sails she saw were still very real to her but they could have turned and gone out into the sea at any time. She paused and treaded water. An especially thick growth of bushes lined the cliff just ahead, dipping down to the very surface of the water. She swam to them and reached out and grasped the outside branches. They moved easily and she pulled back harder. The bush opened wider and Lisa saw the sea flowing through a narrow, tunnel-like opening in the rocks. The opening was wide enough for a rowboat and thoroughly concealed by the bushes that grew over it. She pushed more branches aside and let the water carry her through the entrance. It was pitch black for a few moments and then she saw flickering light glowing ahead. The watery tunnel cut deeply into the rock and she let herself be swept forward, content to float. Suddenly the glow of light grew brighter and she emerged into a wide, sea-level cave, a watery grotto of stone. Three oil lamps flickered on the stone floor of the cave and the water licked the edges of the semicircular grotto. Lisa pulled herself onto the stone and glanced around her in amazement. The cave was crammed with boxes—long boxes, short ones, thick ones, and flat ones. Most of them were open and she saw rifles and what looked to her like automatic weapons jutting up from the boxes. She went over to them and saw that there were many types of guns, some looking like pictures she had seen of self-propelled rocket launchers. There were revolvers and, in the back, stacks of boxes marked AMMUNITION. But mostly there were rifles and though she knew precious little about guns she could make out the Russian markings on those rifles nearest to her. In the foreground, looking terribly incongruous among the deadly weaponry, was a portable, battery-operated record player, very much like one she had at home in Vermont. There was even a record on it.

Lisa glanced around her at the grotto and back at the cache of arms she had discovered. It obviously fitted somehow into the increasingly strange events that had happened but it only made the picture more unclear. She was frowning at her discovery, little pools of water dripping from her onto the stone floor of the grotto, trying to ponder the meaning of it all, when she heard a sound behind her. It was the soft slap of water against a wooden hull and she whirled to see a rowboat emerge from the narrow tunnel into the watery grotto. The lamplight drew coppery shafts from the hair of the man inside it and Lisa gasped. She watched, rooted to the spot, as Michael Barry hopped out of the rowboat beside her, pulling it a few inches out of the water onto the stone. His eyes bored into hers.

"Just what do you think you're doing by this?" he asked, his voice tight. Lisa felt a terrible sadness wrap itself around her as she looked up into his blue eyes. She had made a suspect out of Michael herself, she knew, but now she also knew that she had never really believed it. And now he was here and she felt somehow all hollowed out inside.

"So it was you all along," she finally said, hearing the dryness of her own voice, a dull, flat dryness.

"I don't know what you're talking about," he growled at her.

"You can drop the act," Lisa said, feeling her sadness giving way to gathering anger. He must take her for a complete fool, she thought.

"I'm not even going to argue with you," he said, his lips a tight line. It was an admission of sorts, Lisa told herself. No arguing, just action now.

"When I saw you nosing around the seawall this morning I was certain you were up to something, or at least planning something," he said, glaring at her. "I felt it in my bones so I decided to set up a little watch of my own. Been at it all damned day. When I finally saw you slip into the water and swim off I followed, far enough behind just to keep you in sight."

He turned and pushed the nose of the rowboat back into the water. "I'm getting you out of here first," he said. "I don't want you found in here. I'll take you someplace where you'll be out of the way and I can go on from there."

Lisa grimaced. Someplace where she'd be out of the way. Out of the way meaning dead, she snorted silently. Michael Barry's broad back was to her as he pulled on the rowboat. It was her one chance. If she were going to be taken away to be disposed of she wouldn't just go along quietly. One of the rifles stuck out of a box at her side. She grabbed the barrel of it and swung with all her might. Michael turned to her just as the heavy stock of the rifle slammed into his temple. She saw his eyes glaze as he fell in a crumpled heap at her feet. It was just then that she heard another sound, from the back of the cave, and she whirled to see the man, Kosta, jumping down from a stone ledge onto another, then leaping over a box of ammunition. There was obviously another entrance to the cave from the back. He was running toward her, leaping over boxes, and she saw the deep, ugly gash on his left cheekbone, the kind of gash an andiron would make! A lot of things could begin to make sense if she had the time to fit them together. She started to turn to dive into the water but her foot slipped on the small pool that had dripped from her suit and the wet stone skidded her feet out from under her. Before she could rise he was upon her, one huge hand reaching out, grasping her by the neck. Lisa tried to hit him with the rifle she still clutched but he flung her to one side like a sack of wheat. She saw the corner of the box for a brief instant as she came down on it and then the world exploded into sharp pain, brilliant colors, and then blackness. Dimly she felt herself going limp, the cold stone against her legs and stomach, and then there was no more.

CHAPTER NINE

*"Do not flee the ashes
to fall into the coals."*
—OLD GREEK PROVERB

SHE WAS CONSCIOUS first of the coldness on her legs, against her back, and she felt naked. A gray curtain began to lift from her eyes and she groaned and turned halfway onto her side. Her arm brushed against a narrow strip of cloth and she remembered she wore a bikini and she was not naked. What was she doing wearing a bikini, she asked herself, and she lay still, letting the curtain raise a little more. She had been swimming, of course. Suddenly, as water rushes through floodgates when they're opened, the curtain lifted and memory rushed over her. She opened her eyes and tried to push herself upright. Her hands were acting strangely. Dimly she realized her wrists were bound behind her back. She strained at the bonds, fairly thin cord, and discovered they were really quite loose. Then she looked up to see Michael sitting only a few feet from her, his back against one of the wooden boxes of rifles. She felt her frown deepening as she looked at him. His ankles were bound together with the same cord that tied her wrists, but far tighter, and his hands were tied behind his back too. A terrible sinking sensation gathered in the pit of her stomach.

"Why are you tied up that way?" she asked. His blue eyes flashed sparks at her.

"Because I'm their leader," he snapped. "Don't you know they always keep the leader tied up this way? It's a mark of respect. It means they don't want him to soil his hands doing any work."

The sinking sensation in her stomach had become a leaden ball. "Oh, Michael," she said. "I'm sorry. I'm so sorry." She saw the ugly red bruise on his temple and her heart shriveled up. "I just thought..."

"I know what you thought," he snapped, cutting her off. "Nothing like jumping to conclusions, is there? You've a positive talent for it."

Even here he could infuriate her with his acid shafts and she felt her temper respond. "I said I'm sorry and I am, terribly," she answered. "But it was a perfectly logical conclusion to come to when I saw you come in here after me."

He smiled at her, a smile that was coated with ice.

"Perfectly logical for you," he corrected her and Lisa felt her cheeks color. She lapsed into silence, an angry, hurt, sorry, contrite silence.

"Did I tell you that you look damn good in a bikini?" she heard him say and she looked up to catch his grin.

"Oh, Michael, Michael," she half sobbed. "I'm sorry I didn't have more trust."

"That makes two of us," he said, the moment of tenderness quickly gone, the cool containment in his eyes again.

"Where is Kosta?" Lisa asked and Michael motioned toward the back of the cave with his head.

"Gone back there to bring in someone else, I'll wager," he said. "There must be a small one-man crevice back there."

"What is it all about, Michael?" Lisa asked, her eyes wide. "I know that Kosta was masquerading as the spirit of Athena on the terrace. I gave him that gash on his cheekbone."

At Michael's surprised glance she quickly told him of how she had fought her way down the terrace steps in the fog and what she'd decided afterwards. He shook his head grimly at her when she finished.

"You're a menace, all right," he said.

"But what does it all mean?" Lisa asked. "Why the pretense about being the spirit of Athena? Why the murders?"

"I can give you an educated guess, seeing all this stuff," Michael said. "They've been smuggling arms, Russian arms, into the Arab countries through Syria. Cyprus would make a perfect and logical place to store the shipments en route while details for each shipment were worked out. In these things each shipment is usually a separate transaction. The arms are no doubt brought here from the Turkish coast to the north, smuggled through Turkey from the Russian border in small shipments. They're stored here until enough has arrived for Arab boats from Syria to come out and pick them up."

"That's why they didn't want Maggie to come to Orion Hall?" Lisa asked. "They were afraid we might stumble onto something?"

"More than that, I'd guess," Michael answered. "This crummy old grotto is a temporary thing, I'm sure. They were no doubt using Orion Hall as the storehouse for the shipments and the place for the Arab boats to make the pickups. It was roomy enough and sat right on the water. Even through the fog it could be picked out if anything could and they had to operate under cover of fog. It'd be too risky otherwise."

"But why the pretense about Athena prowling the terrace?" Lisa asked. "And what about the wailing?"

"I think if we could put that portable record player on you'd hear the wailing that came up from the terrace," Michael said. "They knew the old legend about Athena and to make sure that none of the villagers were out prowling about on the nights of the shipments or pickups they used the old legend. They reactivated it, you might say, knowing it wouldn't take much to play upon the superstitions and fears of these people."

"And, of course, when Maggie and I arrived they couldn't stop," Lisa said. "They had added reason to go on, then."

"That's about it, as I put it together now," Michael said.

"A remarkably excellent analysis," a voice said and Lisa turned her head to see Kosta standing there with a smallish man who wore a burnoose over occidental clothing. It was the robed man who had spoken and he stepped forward, closer to them. Lisa and Michael had been so intent on their reconstruction of events that they hadn't heard Kosta and the other man come up, and now, as he stepped more fully into the light of the lamp, Lisa gasped. From beneath the burnoose sharp, ferretlike features peered out at her and small, glittering eyes held hers.

"Burton," she exclaimed. "You're that lawyer from the East End in London."

"I am glad your memory is so good, Miss Bowen," he said, smiling a thin smile that was anything but a smile. "When Kosta told me of you, and how he himself had been shocked at seeing how strikingly like Athena you were, I decided that you might even help us in keeping the people of the village away from Orion Hall. And you have. When you simply disappear, as you will after this, they will be certain you are somewhere about, lurking in the night, the spirit of Athena returned to carry on her search for vengeance. So, while you and your aunt have indeed been a problem, you have also been helpful to us."

"If I don't show up at Orion Hall in the morning Maggie will turn this whole island upside down looking for me," Lisa said, wishing she felt as confident as she sounded.

The little man's smile was chilling in its deadliness.

"No, I doubt that," he said softly. "We will see to it that a message is delivered to her saying you have gone off for the day with this good fellow right here." He pointed to Michael and then, with shocking suddenness, lashed out with his foot and kicked Michael in the stomach. Lisa felt the pain of it herself as Michael fell over on his side.

"And you, my nosy friend, have made your last discovery," the man said. "Word has reached us that you have been snooping into matters which do not concern your archaeological work at all."

Michael righted himself by pushing down with his hands behind his back and Lisa saw the pain still on his face. The smallish man walked over to Lisa and bent down before her. He let his hands travel over her body, slowly, deliberately, enjoying his every touch, and Lisa closed her eyes and set her teeth together as he explored inside her bikini. Finally he stopped and she opened her eyes to stare at him.

"You are quite delectable," he said. "I should like to take you back with me under other circumstances. I am sure you could give me much pleasure. But, unfortunately, your disappearance might cause trouble and we must be very careful. It will be dawn soon. You will be held here until tomorrow night. We can't risk moving you in the daylight. Then tomorrow night an accident will be arranged for you."

"Yes, you're big on accidents," Lisa said sharply. The man nodded. "As I said, we operate very carefully. There is a lot at stake. You and your aunt have been very difficult to discourage and you have been very lucky. But your luck has run out, as they say in your country."

He turned and took Kosta aside, speaking to the big, cavernous-eyed man in muffled tones. Finally he turned to Lisa again.

"Do not be so foolish as to try to escape," he said. "Kosta would welcome the chance to kill you himself. But he is here to guard you until night when others will come to take you. It will be a simple matter to get rid of your aunt, then. And we must hurry with that. We expect a large shipment and we need the room in Orion Hall."

He turned abruptly, kicked Michael again as he walked by, and disappeared into the back of the cave with Kosta.

"Nice chap," Michael gasped through his pain.

"It's all my fault," Lisa sobbed, the tears erupting all of a sudden. "If I hadn't hit you we might have gotten out of here. And if I hadn't gone and come here on my own you wouldn't have followed me."

"True, all true," she heard him say. "Every word of it." She glared at him through her sobs. He didn't have to make her feel worse by agreeing so with her.

"You didn't expect me to sooth your little feelings, did you?" Michael snapped at her. Lisa's jaw tightened. Dammit, it was amazing how he could make her temper flare.

"No, I guess not," she retorted. "That would have been out of character."

"Definitely," he said as she glared at him. She had been emotionally collapsing in a basket of self-recriminations and depression but now she knitted her brows together in angry determination.

"Maybe we're not finished yet," she said in a low voice. "Maggie might believe the message they'll get to her but someone else will wonder about it when he stops at the house."

Michael frowned. "Go on," he said.

"Demetrius," Lisa said and Michael's lips pursed in thought.

"I see," he said quietly. "At least I think I do. He'll wonder how come you've gone off for the day with me when you and he have been getting on so well. That's it, right?"

Lisa felt the warm flush spreading across her face. "Something like that," she said.

Michael's voice was bland, dry. "Let's hope it works," he said. Lisa nodded. She wasn't as sure as she had sounded. Demetrius might not have returned. Or he might not stop at the house till later in the day. But mostly she feared that he might get the message and be too hurt to do anything but go back to his place. Perhaps Michael had the same fears, she wondered, as he spoke to her in quiet, urgent tones.

"Listen carefully to me, Lisa," he said. "Kosta will be back in a few moments. They've got me tied good and tight but I notice they only tied your wrists and perhaps not too good a job of that." Lisa nodded. "We're going to be here all day, waiting. I want you to spend every minute you can working on your wrist bonds. Sit against the box, rub them on it, keep working on them, loosening them."

"Yes," she said eagerly. "I think they'll come loose in time. But what then?"

"You dive into the water and start swimming. Get out of here," he said. "Kosta will still be alone, or we're out of luck. But if he is he won't be able to follow you and watch me at the same time. I know his type of mentality. He'll stick with the bird he's got in the hand, in this case me."

"But what will happen to you?"

"That will depend on how fast you get back here with the authorities," Michael said. "I hope nothing will happen to me. I'm really not the hero type."

His eyes twinkled at her. "Get started on those ropes," he said and Lisa nodded. She shifted her body so that she leaned back against one of the long boxes. The open lock pressed against her wrists and she rubbed the cord against its sharp edge, working deliberately and very slowly. Kosta returned and took up a position halfway around the perimeter of the semicircle and this time, Lisa noted, he held a rifle in his hands. His piercing eyes lingered frequently on her body and she was grateful that she wasn't to be left to his mercies. By night others would come to take her and kill her. Kosta would, she was sure, make death more torturous and lingering. The gaunt-faced man was content to sit at his place with only an occasional walk to check more closely on his captives. During those times, or when she saw him raise his head to devour her with his eyes, she would sit perfectly still. Then, at the first chance, she would return to rubbing the wrist bonds across the edge of the latch. It was painfully slow and her wrists were beginning to cramp up from the unnatural movement, her shoulder muscles ached and tightened, and her pauses became more and more frequent. No daylight filtered into the gloom of the watery grotto but both she and Michael knew that the morning had gone into afternoon and they were still captives. No one had come to save them and as the hours dragged on she knew it had been a foolish thought in the first place. Even if Demetrius had become alarmed and alerted the authorities no one could find this sea-level cave without some lead to its existence. No, there would be no one coming to save them unless she got free. Looking across at Michael, seeing the encouragement in his eyes, she knew that he had no doubt realized that from the very beginning. He merely hadn't said anything to depress her and instead had had her start trying to get free. With renewed desperation she moved the wrist cords against the metal edge of the lock.

"It will be dark soon," Michael said. "I've been keeping pretty good count of the time in my head. You won't have more than three hours left after night falls. They won't come to take you out of here until they're certain the whole village is shut down for the night. That would make it about midnight, I'd guess." Then, his voice dropping almost inaudibly, he spoke again.

"Do you feel anything giving?" he asked her.

"I think so," she whispered. "I ought to know soon." But the time began to change from slow to swift as the night and what it would bring began to peer over each second. Michael kept his glances of bright encouragement going her way but Lisa saw the increasing tension in his face. Disregarding her cramped, aching muscles she jammed the wrist cords against the metal and with surprising suddenness she felt her hands come apart. She pulled again and the cord shredded and she was free. It was an automatic reaction as she pulled her hands free to bring her arms up. Kosta glanced up just as she did. His piercing eyes widened and he started to his feet in surprise as Michael yelled at her.

"Go Lisa, now!" Michael shouted. Kosta was starting to run toward her, the rifle in his hand. Lisa cast a glance at Michael who yelled again at her and then she dived, her long, slender body knifing into the circle of water at the foot of the grotto floor. She struck out for the bottom as she heard Kosta's angry yell, lost as the swirl of water closed over her head. But the sound of the shot stayed with her and so did the heavy thump of the bullet as it struck the water only inches from her. She stayed down and started for the narrow tunnel entrance, knowing the man above was waiting to see her surface and to shoot again. She felt the walls of the cave come together to form the tunnel and she swam through the narrow opening below the surface, finally coming up midway through it, far from Kosta's eyes and his rifle. She swam with every ounce of her strength now, knowing what she had to do to save Michael. Pushing her way through the outside covering of bushes she found herself out in the darkness of the night, the moon still hardly more than a suggestion in the sky. Her arms rose up and down in the dark as she swam furiously once more along the shoreline, under the shadows of the towering cliffs, her mind racing as she swam. The only authority she knew of in the tiny village was the dour mayor and she would have to raise him out of his bed and try to explain what it was all about. That could take an hour. Or, the thought arose, her story might be disbelieved. Or put off till the morning for further discussion. It was a more than likely possibility, one she could not risk.

There was Maggie, of course. But that would mean explaining things to her and then the older woman wouldn't really know any other place to go for help than the mayor. She'd be back in the same situation, rousing him and risking his skeptical disbelief. No, the one chance was Demetrius and she prayed he had indeed returned from his trip and was at his place, at the little white-washed house. The towering cliff sides began to slope abruptly and she saw the village quay just ahead to her left. She reached it and pulled herself up onto the white stone, lying there for a moment to regain her breath and find new strength in her aching muscles. But when she got to her feet she ran like a deer in the night, the warm wind drying her body as she crossed the market square behind the waterfront, cut through a narrow, black street, and raced onto the wider street where Demetrius lived. The house, like all the others, was dark and silent. She pushed on the door and it opened and she stood in an inky black hallway. But there was a door to the right and a yellow glow of light came from under it. She went to it and called in a half whisper: "Demetrius! Demetrius, it's me, Lisa."

She heard a sound inside the room and the door was flung open. Demetrius stood there, wearing trousers but no shirt. His handsome countenance wore a look of absolute shock as his eyes bored into her and she suddenly realized what an incongruous picture she made standing there in the bikini.

"Lisa!" he finally said. "What in the name of Zeus are you doing here? I was told you had gone away for the day."

"No." Lisa shook her head quickly. "I've been held prisoner." The words tumbled from her in wild profusion as she told him what had happened, tugging at his arm all the while. She began with her discovery that the spirit of Athena was something of flesh and blood and went on from there.

"When I found the cave I swam in through a small tunnel opening," she said. "It was full of guns and ammunition. That was when Michael Barry came in. He'd followed me and he was made prisoner too. They are a band of men smuggling arms from Russia to the Arab countries. They've been using Orion Hall as a station between the Turkish border and Syria. Kosta is one of them and so is an Arab I met in London who posed as a lawyer using the name Al Burton. And there are others who are coming to take me away tonight and kill me in one of their carefully arranged *accidents*. Oh, Demetrius, you've got to help me. Come on, I'll tell you more on the way."

Demetrius' hand closed on her arm and he hurried out to the street with her. Outside, he glanced up and down quickly.

"The town's asleep," Lisa said. "What can we do? Wake up the mayor? Is there a police force here?"

"No, he would have to call men from Yialousa and that would take time, too much time," Demetrius said. "Whatever we do will have to be done by us alone."

"The boats bringing the guns in and out use the sea tunnel entrance," Lisa said. "But there's some kind of small entrance in the back of the cave, from the cliffs. I know I can find the area if you think we could find the back entrance."

"We'll find it," Demetrius said grimly. "I have a small car I keep at the end of the village in an empty lot. We can take it up to the cliff area at least and search the rest of the way on foot."

Lisa's heart soared and she hugged Demetrius as they started to run down the street, his hand still holding tightly to her wrist. The car in the empty lot was an open-topped old English sport car that had seen better days. Lisa slipped into the seat beside Demetrius. The sound of the engine starting in the silent night was frightening. Demetrius swung the car from the lot and started out of town.

"You told no one else of your suspicions about all this before you left to go searching on your own?" he asked. "No one else we can pick up and bring along for help, I mean?"

"Nobody," Lisa answered. "We could go back and get Maggie. She'd come."

"No," he said, the line of his jaw tight, angry. "She would only be in the way." He swung the car around a sharp curve on two wheels. "And Michael Barry," Demetrius pressed, "you say he was all alone when he followed you. He said nothing about anyone else when he woke up?"

"No, he didn't," Lisa said, and then her heart stopped. Choking horror leaped up inside her, sickening disbelief. The world spun crazily, never to be the same again, she knew. Her eyes turned to stare at Demetrius, a terrible pain filling her chest.

"I didn't say anything about Michael waking up," she said, her voice barely a whisper. "I didn't tell you I'd hit him and knocked him out."

Demetrius turned toward her. His lips formed a smile that was not really a smile at all. "Of course you did, Lisa," he said softly. "You're so excited you don't remember what you said."

"No, I remember," Lisa said, her voice still an anguished whisper. "I didn't say anything at all about it."

She hadn't mentioned it, not a word of it, she knew. Only Kosta had seen her hit Michael with the rifle. Only he could have told the man, Burton, and only Burton could have told it to Demetrius.

"You're one of them," she heard herself say, the horror of it enveloping her even tighter. "You're their leader, aren't you?"

Suddenly, like jumping jacks popping up in their individual boxes, all sorts of things were popping up in her mind, revealing themselves for what they really were.

"The sunbonnet was something to mark me for death," she said, her voice strained, tight. "And of course you were so shocked to see me afterwards. You'd been told the girl in the sunbonnet had been crushed to death. And your sympathetic belief in old legends was to encourage me to believe in the legend of Athena. You told me to wait for a sign, hoping I'd take it and give you another chance to kill me in the fog. Only that turned out a little differently than you'd planned. Even your concern, your kisses, were meant to make me care enough to do whatever you asked."

Her voice broke and she turned away for a moment When she looked back at Demetrius his face was cold stone, the cold, unyielding marble of Greek statues. "Bunglers!" he muttered. "Bunglers and damfools, I'm surrounded with them. But this

THE MISTRESS OF ORION HALL

time I'll take care of things personally." He turned to her, his full lips a harsh scar across his face, and his hand shot out to seize her wrist again. With a cry of pain and fury Lisa flung herself out of the car, tearing her wrist from his grip. She hit the ground and felt her body shudder in pain, thankful it was only a dirt road. She shook her head to clear it and stumbled to her feet. She was running by the time the car stopped, back toward the village, cutting through the trees of a lemon grove alongside the road. She heard Demetrius coming after her, cursing, growling, raging. But in the freedom of the bikini she ran swift as a wraith in the night, dodging in and out of trees. She cut through a small cluster of them and then out to the road again as it reached the beginnings of town. A short gasp escaped her as the big form appeared in front of her. He had left the lemon grove and raced down the road, anticipating she would come back to it where it reached into the village. She tried to dodge but his strong arms seized her and flung her to the ground. He was atop her instantly, his hands forcing her arms back, his face a furious mask.

"They'll be waiting for me to arrive with final instructions," he snarled. "I'll bring them more than they expect this time." He moved, shifting his grip, and yanked her to her feet. There was a brief moment of opportunity and Lisa sank her teeth deep into Demetrius' wrist, tasting the warm blood she drew. He cried out in pain, his hand automatically opening, and she was off and running again. The streets of Caramania beckoned her, twisting, dark, and narrow. She ran up one and down the other, fear lending speed to her legs. He was chasing after her but she knew there was no help here in this sleeping village. Her legs were carrying her to Orion Hall and she realized she was fleeing to the great gargoyle of a house, as Michael had called it, for protection, just as Athena had done on that night long ago. Maggie would be asleep and waking her would only delay her flight, Lisa knew. She glanced back as she raced down the last street toward the house looming up darkly before her. He was gaining on her now, but the great oaken door was just in front of her. She swung it open and raced into the house.

Demetrius roared in after her and she made no effort to hide her movements. There was no time for stealth and she was fleeing, being led more by a strange, instinctual force than by conscious reasoning. And yet her mind was racing as swiftly as her legs. She knew that the face of death had been unmasked finally, and the moment had come at last. She was pulling on the bolt of the east turret door, frantically tugging at it, as Demetrius rushed at her. She flung the door open in his face, ducked under his arm grasping for her, and raced up the curved steps inside the turret. The door had struck him and knocked him back for a moment but he was following her now, his heavy footsteps echoing in the round walls of the turret. She ran, her long, slender legs taking the steps two at a time, beauty pursued by death. Athena's room loomed up before her as she reached the landing. She paused, reached into the door, and found one of the heavy candle pieces. There was no time to light it nor had she the materials. As the dark form of Demetrius reached the landing she swung her arm in a wide arc, flinging the heavy candlestick into his handsome face. She heard it smash and the cry of anger and pain that followed as he staggered back. He dropped to one knee in the near pitch dark but she saw in despair that the blow had not ended it. Lisa leaped past the form on one knee and ran up the rest of the curving steps.

By now Maggie would be aroused, wondering what was happening, she knew. Probably Nikos too. Demetrius, cursing and calling to her now, was coming up the steps. She flung open the door to the balcony atop the turret and stepped outside. The wind struck her near-naked body with the force of a giant slap and she shivered. She moved from the door and looked back at it as Demetrius emerged, dark streaks of blood running down the. side of his face. The classic, handsome face was now a livid snarl of rage, as though a piece of beautiful sculpture had been broken and put together incorrectly. Lisa moved backwards slowly, her hand on the low railing of the turret. Demetrius came toward her, his teeth bared.

"You have made it easy for me," he said hoarsely. "Easy." He charged and Lisa ran, racing around the circular balcony, her fists clenched tightly, hoping desperately she could remember. He was almost on her now. Then, where the stone railing dipped, she leaped forward, landing on the balls of her feet. She whirled and faced Demetrius. He ran toward her and her eyes went to the balcony stones and she saw him come down heavily, saw the stone snap downward on its swivel-like base, saw his body pitch forward in an uncontrolled arc. She closed her eyes as he hit the low wall of the turret and hurtled over it out into the blackness of the night. But she couldn't close out the scream that tore the darkness, echoing up to end suddenly, abruptly, in the finality of sudden death. It was a high-pitched scream, a cry of terror, carrying in it all the fearful realization that the cycle had been completed, that the past had caught up to extract payment in full. It had sounded very much the same a long time ago, she knew. Or was it only yesterday?

Lisa stepped carefully over the stone and went down the black, curving stairs inside the turret. Maggie was in the corridor with Nikos when she reached the bottom, both of them holding lighted lamps.

"My God, what happened to you?" Maggie asked, aghast.

"I'll explain on the way," Lisa said. "You've got to help me. You too, Nikos." Lisa already had the plan loosely formed. In fact, it had taken its own shape when Demetrius told her the others would be waiting for him to bring final instructions. It had taken shape, probably, because it was the only thing left that they could do. Rousing the mayor and all it entailed was no more feasible than it had been before.

"Guns, I need guns, Nikos," Lisa said to the old man. "Do you know where there are any guns?"

He nodded and told her he had four guns in his room. He used to hunt a lot and collect guns, before the sight in his one eye began to fail him. As she and Maggie hurried after Nikos she told them both what had taken place.

"I can't believe it," Maggie finally said when she'd finished. "But it's got to be true. You couldn't make up anything so fantastic. And I certainly did hear that scream just now."

"They're waiting for him in the cave," Lisa said. "They know I've escaped, of course. But they don't know if I really made it. Kosta's shot might have hit me. They're sitting there on pins and needles, waiting for Demetrius to show. They know he'll be raging when he hears what they have to tell him. Our one chance is to make them think that the game is up. We'll go to the cave and start shooting from the tunnel. We'll make it sound like the whole Cyprus police force is about to descend. I'm counting on human nature being what it is. I'm banking that they'll run for that back entrance and get out of there as fast as they can, figuring that it's run or be caught."

"And they won't bother about Michael," Maggie said.

"They'll be too busy trying to get out with their own skins," Lisa said. "In the morning we'll tell the authorities in Yialousa and they can take it from there."

Nikos appeared with the four guns, handing one to Maggie, one to Lisa, and keeping the other two himself. There was an old bolt-action repeater, a heavy shotgun, and two smaller game rifles. "They'll have to do," Lisa said. She started out and the others followed, hurrying through the dark streets to the quay. She took the first rowboat moored there. While Maggie sat in the back, she and Nikos shared the burden of rowing. The tall cliffs rose up quickly as they made fast time and Lisa searched the darkness for the thick bushes that dipped to the water's edge.

CHAPTER TEN

"Next year's wine is the sweetest."
—Cypriote Greek Proverb

Nikos turned out to have more of the old fox in him than she had imagined. As Lisa gestured to the dark stretch of bushes he shipped the oars and began to paddle with his hands. The rowboat moved through the water silently with no sound of creaking oars and passed into the dark tunnel as Lisa held the bushes apart. She had the shotgun in her lap and she glanced at her companions. They made as incongruous and unformidable an attacking force as one could ever think to see: a slender girl in a bikini, a middle-aged dowager, and an old one-eyed man. The boat moved into the narrow tunnel and she held it from scraping the sides with her hands. The glimmer of the oil lamps in the cave flickered ahead of them.

"Get ready," Lisa whispered. They had to start firing before the boat reached the wide interior and they could be seen. Lisa raised the shotgun, glanced back at Maggie who was crouched on one knee, and stretched out on the floor so the older woman could fire over her.

"Now!" she whispered. Nikos shot first, Maggie second, and Lisa fired the heavy shotgun last. They continued shooting at once and the tunnel seemed to explode with the sound of the shots. It sounded like there were cannons in the attacking force as the little grotto reverberated with the explosions. The echoes bouncing off the walls made it impossible to tell how many shots were actually being fired. Lisa smiled as she heard the shouts from inside but her smile froze as she thought of what would happen if they decided not to run. They had an arsenal in there to fight with. The rowboat drifted forward and they were almost at the end of the tunnel, about to emerge. She heard the sounds of men cursing and running and she took a deep breath. Nikos was reloading but Lisa waved a hand at him. The cave was still except for the reverberations that still echoed in it as the little boat drifted into the circle of light. Michael was where she had last seen him, still bound hand and foot, his back against a box of rifles. She saw his eyes widen in astonishment as the boat bumped against the cave floor.

"I'll be damned," he said. "That's all there is, just you?"

"That's all there is," Lisa laughed as she hopped from the boat. Nikos followed her and brought out a fishing knife to cut Michael's bonds. Michael still stared at the trio in disbelief as he got to his feet, rubbing circulation back into his wrists.

"In 53 B.C., at Carrhae, the Parthians with their archers destroyed thirty thousand Roman legionnaires," he said. "They should have had you three along."

He turned to Lisa standing close to him. "Thanks for coming back," he said, his eyes serious.

"You came after me to save me," she said, quietly, and suddenly his arms were holding her to him. It felt good and safe and very right.

"Naturally," he said. "I've other plans for you."

"I'm glad," she said and without warning she felt very light-headed and dizzy and all that had happened swept back over her. "Something went wrong, didn't it?" Michael asked and she nodded. She told him of Demetrius in halting words, choking back tears that were made of delayed reactions to all that had taken place. "Let's get you back," Michael said. "It's time you got out of that bikini anyway. We'll talk more later."

Lisa nodded and stepped into the boat with him. She felt very small, very drained of all emotion. Nikos rowed back and they were at the quay before dawn touched the sky. Michael's hands were comforting at her waist, his eyes understanding as they reached Orion Hall. She fell into bed with Maggie throwing a cover over her naked form, the bikini cast aside on the floor beside the bed. She slept deeply, far into the morning, and when she woke the sun was hot and high. She turned and felt her nakedness under the covers and she thought of Michael and another time not long ago. She got up, a secret smile edging her lips, bathed quickly, dressed, and hurried downstairs.

He was there, waiting for her, his blue eyes surveying her with that calm, contained light. All the proper authorities had been informed, he told her, and the contents of the cave already confiscated.

"A lot of old legends were put to rest last night," he said. She regarded him with grave eyes. He was right but there were still things untouched.

"But I knew things without knowing, Michael," she said. "That hasn't changed. The pomegranates and the terrace steps, the way I felt about Orion Hall, all those unexplained things."

He came closer to her and put his hand under her chin and now his eyes were serious, unsmiling.

"They're going to stay that way, Lisa," he said, "until we learn more than we now know about what makes this thing we call life. Some people have coined terms for such things. They call the study of phenomena which defy rational explanation parapsychology. It takes in clairvoyance, telepathy, and contacts with the past and the future. It's interesting that even there the old Greeks get into the act. The prefix *para* is from the Greek, meaning beyond or beside or something aside from the usual. Parapsychology is a rational study on a scientific basis of irrational and unscientific things. But the mere fact that we study these things admits that we recognize the existence of them. Some of us never experience them. Others often do. You did and no one on earth can explain it to you. Psychic communication exists. We merely don't understand it or how it functions or on what levels."

"But if you let yourself believe in these things, in the unknown forces behind them, when do you stop believing?" Lisa asked. "Do you believe then in the power of evil? Do you believe in witches and old spells and things that carry over forever and ever?"

"Don't believe in anything that can't be proven," Michael said, his eyes smiling at her. "But don't disbelieve in it either."

"That's a lot of help," Lisa said in annoyance. He shrugged, his eyes laughing at her again.

"You know what you felt," he said. "You know what happened. You'll have to wrestle with what to believe in on your own. Of course you'll need help from someone experienced in separating legend from reality."

"I see," Lisa said, her eyes holding his. "Like a trained archaeologist?"

"Perfect choice," he said. He pulled her to him and his lips were parting hers, strong yet sweet, and a delicious warmth flooded through her veins. It was physical communication of a high order. Finally Lisa pulled away and looked up at Michael. He grinned down at her.

"You take a long time to realize things," he commented.

"Is that so?" she snapped. "And when did you know you felt this way?"

"About a minute and a half after I saw you falling down that hillside," he said. "I knew you felt it too."

"How did you know that?" she asked, frowning.

"You kept getting angry at me," he grinned. "It's a sure sign."

"Living with you would be insufferable," Lisa snapped.

"But fun," Michael said, and she felt herself laughing, knowing he was right. "But fun," she echoed, throwing her arms around him.

Maggie came into the corridor and was the first to know and she was happy for them both. The authorities had assured her that living at Orion Hall would be without trouble from now on. Lisa stayed on with her for another week while Michael packed and crated his "diggings," as he called them. Maggie and Nikos went to Kyrenia to see them off on the old steamer. Lisa let her eyes sweep the port and the island of Cyprus as it receded in the distance, sun swept and picture-book fresh. She had come to Kyrenia and she had entered the walls. And she had stayed long enough but she hadn't gotten married there. That she and Michael had agreed would happen in the hills of Vermont, and soon. If the gypsy woman was on the dock when they landed in Athens she would tell her so.